Brody grabbed his tools and winked at her. 2017

"Seems silly for you to get cleaned up only to get dirty again..." she said.

Dirty. Why did everything out of Mari's mouth sound like sexual innuendo?

Because of the kiss and you were tight against Brody's—

Stop it.

She pushed away the thoughts of stripping off his tank and running her hands across his tight abs. Far, far away.

"Right. Tile." She gestured toward the staircase, so that he could get started.

"Cool." He stepped past her and headed on up. "Where am I going?"

"Bathroom. Second door on the right." The man's butt as he climbed the stairs was a sight to behold.

No, this wasn't going to be a bad idea at all...

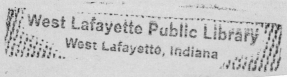

Dear Reader,

This story, along with the two more in this series, was inspired by a group of Marines I saw in the airport in Dallas one day. They were sitting around—men and women, laughing and giving each other a hard time. Turns out they were heading home (I might have eavesdropped a little). I don't know where they'd been, but it sent my imagination into overdrive, and I started writing furiously in my notebook.

I also have an addiction to HGTV. And those two things, the Marines and remodeling a house, sort of came together in my head. That's how Brody came to be the handsome Marine who lives across the street from Mari, the heroine. While he's far from perfect, he can fix almost anything—maybe even Mari's broken heart.

I'd like to thank those Marines for inspiring me, and to all of the servicemen and women who put their lives on the line to protect our freedom.

I would love to hear from you. You can follow me on Twitter, @candacehavens, and Facebook, facebook.com/pages/candace-havens, or visit me at candacehavens.com.

Candace

Candace Havens

Her Sexy Marine Valentine

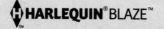

Recycling programs
for this product may
not exist in your area.

ISBN-13: 978-0-373-79887-2

Her Sexy Marine Valentine

Copyright © 2016 by Candace Havens

Printed in U.S.A.

Candace "Candy" Havens is a bestselling and award-winning author. She is a two-time RITA® Award, Write Touch Reader and Holt Medallion finalist. She is also a winner of the Barbara Wilson Award. Candy is a nationally syndicated entertainment columnist for FYI Television. A veteran journalist, she has interviewed just about everyone in Hollywood. You can hear Candy weekly on New Country 96.3 KSCS in the Dallas-Fort Worth Area.

Books by Candace Havens

Harlequin Blaze

Take Me If You Dare
She Who Dares, Wins
Truth and Dare
Her Last Best Fling

Uniformly Hot!

Model Marine
Mission: Seduction

To get the inside scoop on Harlequin Blaze and its talented writers, be sure to check out BlazeAuthors.com.

All backlist available in ebook format.

Visit the Author Profile page at Harlequin.com for more titles.

Jill Marsal, thank you for your patience and for hangin' tight. You are awesomeness.

1

LIEUTENANT BRODY WILLIAMS dumped a bag of tortilla chips in his grocery cart and tried not to wince when the wheels squeaked. The headaches were less intense since the crash, but he still had them daily. That level of pain, paired with the dreams that had him waking up in the middle of the night in a cold sweat, had left him feeling rotten for months. If he took the drugs the doctors gave him, he couldn't fly, so he ran for miles every day and drank more coffee than any man should.

He added salsa to his cart. A hobby, that's what he needed, something that would keep him busy and the memories at bay. Fixing up his rented house was almost complete. New projects—that would do it. He was about to turn the corner when he saw the familiar red head.

Shoot. His CO's daughter was walking down the frozen food section.

Why does she always seem to turn up wherever I am?

He'd met her at a reception his boss threw a few weeks ago. At first, he'd thought she was pretty, but then discovered she was the boss's daughter. Hands off that one. Unfortunately, she didn't seem to understand that dating her wasn't even a remote possibility for him. His boss was already an aggravation, he didn't need to be adding to it by taking out the man's daughter.

Turning his cart quickly, he headed the opposite way. A woman plus a couple were blocking his escape. He stood off to one side pretending to look at the different brands of coffee.

"Marigold, I'd like you to meet my beautiful fiancée, Annalise. She's a model," the man said. "She's been in a ton of magazines." His tone was snide and Brody felt sorry for Marigold.

"Fiancée? But we only broke up two months ago," she said. "I mean, congrats and all, but that's kind of fast." The voice was familiar to Brody, smooth and rich like honey.

The guy was showing off his new girl to his ex? From Marigold's reaction, she was barely holding on by a thread. Brody's guess was that this guy had done a real number on her. And she was right. A couple of months wasn't nearly long enough to get to know someone well enough to marry them. Heck, twenty years wasn't long enough in his book. Then again, he never planned on marrying.

He sucked at relationships. Mostly because he

was seldom in one place for longer than six months. As a pilot, and a trainer, his situation could change any day.

"Oh, my little sweetie couldn't wait to put a ring on it," the woman named Annalise said, as she waved her hand back and forth. Brody realized he knew the poor woman who was caught in her ex's crosshairs. She was his neighbor, Mari, or rather Marigold. He'd once lugged some wood flooring she'd been struggling with. She said she was flipping the old Victorian across the street from his place. He'd wondered then why she didn't have someone to give her a hand with heavy loads like the flooring. Not that he minded helping. She'd been kind and even offered him lemonade.

That day she'd been wearing a ball cap pulled low, and baggy overalls and a fresh white tank, but those deep blue eyes had made him think about the sea off the coast of Greece. Today, her shiny blond hair was pulled up into a sleek ponytail and she wore denim shorts with a Dallas Cowboys jersey. He could forgive her choice of team, if only because of the startled look in her eyes.

He hadn't been able to help his men a year ago. He'd barely been able to help himself, but he could do something about this.

"Mari, there you are," he said before he even realized the words were coming out of his mouth. He pushed around her ex. "I've been looking all over for you, babe. I found the chips and salsa, but not the cheese stuff you wanted."

At first, she glanced up at him as if he was crazy, but then she smiled when she recognized him.

That smile stole his breath away. As in, he could not suck in air even if he tried. Damn. She was beautiful.

She cleared her throat. "That's okay, honey, I think I'll make the *queso* from scratch," she said without missing a beat. Then she stood on her toes and kissed his cheek. Her lips were soft. "I love that you are so helpful." And then in his ear she whispered, "Thank you."

"You know I'd do anything for you." He grabbed her and pulled her to him. Her vanilla scent made him forget where they were. "Who's this? Do I need to be jealous?" He nodded toward her ex.

"Oh, uh…" She stumbled over the words. "My ex. He was introducing me to his fiancée."

The other man appeared as if he'd swallowed a toad. Clearly he hadn't been expecting Mari to find a man so quickly.

Brody chuckled. "Well, I should take you out to dinner, man. Because if you hadn't been an idiot and left my Mari, my life would be empty. She's the best thing that has ever happened to me. The day we met was the most special one in my life." Oh, now he was laying it on thick, but he couldn't stop. He had this need to protect her. To show this fool what he was missing. The brunette with the false eyelashes and even falser breasts couldn't compare to the natural beauty he held in his arms.

The ex's mouth opened and then closed, as if he couldn't decide what to say. His brows furrowed and he opened his mouth again, but...

The brunette squealed. "I've had a marvelous idea. You guys have to come to our engagement party," she said. "It's so cool that everyone can kind of be bygones."

Wow. He had a feeling the supposed model had no idea what *bygones* meant.

"That's probably not a marvelous idea," the ex said. "I'm sure they're busy."

"We do stay pretty busy," Mari said.

"True," Brody agreed. "But send us an invite anyway. You never know. I love showing off my Mari."

The jerk's eyes flashed wide. Good. Even if she didn't go, he'd be worried she might show up.

"We should get going," Mari said. She put a hand on his arm and shot him a quick grin. "I hope you two will be very happy together. Come on, Brody."

He and Mari turned and made it several aisles over before stopping. "You didn't have to do that, but thank you," she said softly. She blew out a breath. "That wasn't how I imagined seeing him for the first time since we broke up. I was shocked. I mean, who gets engaged so fast? We dated for five years."

"You're better off without him," Brody said honestly. "And you're way too good for him."

She grinned. "You've known me five seconds, but thank you. It was really kind. The breakup was bad and I thought I was over it, but wow. Just wow. You're the best. I was sinking there and you threw me a life preserver."

He still wasn't sure why he'd done it. Wasn't like him to butt into a stranger's business. He preferred being alone. But there was something about her that made him want to get involved. "It's a Marine thing. We live by our code. You were a damsel in distress and I came to your aid."

"I'm not sure anyone, especially someone I didn't know well, has ever been so kind to me. I'd say your duty is done, Marine. That was just a whole lot of awesome. He looked like a marooned fish trying to figure out what to say." She laughed this time. It was a sweet sound. "You are the *best* boyfriend ever."

"Brody?"

His shoulders tightened at the sound of his name. She'd finally found him. "Please help me," he whispered to Mari before turning around.

"Hey, Carissa."

The CO's daughter had her eyebrow raised and seemed to be focused on something, or rather someone, just past his shoulder.

"Did I hear you say you're dating her?" She pointed a red fingernail toward Mari.

"Do you have a problem with that?" Mari said. Her acidic tone very nearly made him chuckle.

Knowing a cue when he heard one, he quickly stepped aside and grabbed her hand. It was so small in his, and her skin was silky smooth against his calloused mitts. He raised Mari's fingers to his lips and kissed them. "Calm down, babe. This is my CO's daughter, Carissa. The *boss's* daughter."

"Oh. Ohhhh." She smiled and then shook her head. "I'm so sorry. Hi, I'm Marigold McDaniels. You have to forgive me. My man is so handsome that I always have to be on alert to discourage women from throwing themselves at him. It gets annoying after a while. But he's a sweetheart, and I'm maybe just a little bit the jealous type. At least, when it comes to Brody."

Mari might win an award some day for this performance.

For once Carissa seemed speechless, but still, she recovered quickly. "Funny that he's never mentioned you."

"That's my fault," Mari said. "It's so new between us, and I got out of a really bad relationship not that long ago. Like horrifically bad. So we haven't been telling people, until, well, today. We just ran in to my ex."

"Awkward," Brody said in a singsong voice. That didn't sound like him at all; it caught him off guard. Maybe he'd be the one winning the award. And if this charade of theirs kept the CO's daughter from hitting on him in the future, he'd owe Mari for life. "I kind of wanted to punch his lights out for hurting my Mari." That part was true. He'd never wanted to smack a guy so bad. "But at the same time, if he hadn't been so dumb, Mari and I would never have met."

"Huh." Carissa gave them a weak smile. "Well, my dad will be glad to hear you're putting down some roots finally. In fact, you should bring her to the picnic on Saturday. It will be good for you to socialize, get to know more people. Dad's still trying to build camaraderie and teamwork hopefully by bringing folks together off base," Carissa said to Mari. "He's mentioned several times that Brody seems to be a bit of a loner."

Why would the boss be discussing him with Carissa? Brody wasn't happy to hear that.

He'd forgotten about the team-building events. He didn't understand why simply doing the job wasn't enough anymore. They were Marines. Being smart and self-reliant were the important qualities to have. Not worrying about connecting with others and all that stuff. You interacted with one another, sure, but everyone had to focus and do their own job.

He glanced down at pretty Mari. Shoot. The last thing Brody needed in his life was a woman. A relationship only meant complications. Once you cared about someone—

"Babe, you promised we could lay wood," Mari said, with a giggle and a sexy smile on her lips. Parts of his body reacted. This woman was definitely dangerous if merely her laugh could make him hard. "Sorry. What I mean is we're supposed to put the wood floors down on Saturday."

He gently tugged her ponytail. "You're a bad, bad girl." She was funny and quick, as well as beautiful. Yep, a wicked combination. "I always keep my promises, but maybe we can figure out how to do both." He leaned down and kissed her cheek. He had to, she smelled so good, looked so good and… right, Carissa was watching. He knew there was another reason. He admitted it was hard to think when Mari was smiling up at him like that.

"You've got that look again." She rolled her eyes. "But I can never tell if you want food or—"

Her. Naked. In his bed.

What was that? His imagination was in overdrive.

Food. He needed to eat, or maybe it was the headache. It was causing him to hallucinate.

"You. Babe, when it comes to a choice between food or you, it's always going to be you."

"Uh, right. Well, I believe that's the sign for me to leave," Carissa said, "but you two might want to get a room. The grocery aisle isn't the place for that sort of thing, and I'm pretty open-minded. So we'll see you both on Saturday." With that she sauntered off.

Finally. He relaxed. But then he realized he was still holding on to Mari's shoulders. He reluctantly let go.

"That was fun. We should start a theater group or something." She chuckled.

"It was. Thanks for coming to my rescue. She's been asking me out since I arrived at the base. I do a lot of stupid stuff, I confess, but messing around with the CO's daughter is not on the list."

"I can tell she's used to men saying yes, so you must be quite the challenge. She's superattractive, though."

He shrugged. "Not my type. You have no idea how grateful I am to you right now. She's too much, a real piece of work."

"I should be thanking you," Mari said. "In fact, let me make you dinner. A man cannot live on tortilla chips and salsa alone." She pointed at his cart. "And I was making tacos anyway. We could combine our resources and have a great meal."

A home-cooked meal didn't sound so bad. It had been a while. He could cook, but doing it for one person always seemed a waste.

Though sharing a meal with Mari might not be the best idea. In just the few minutes they'd spent together, he'd become very attracted to her. And that was not a good thing. Better to let her down easy. "You don't have to do that, we helped each other out."

"I know, but I want to and I…" She stared down at her feet as if she were afraid to say whatever was coming next.

"What?" he asked.

"I have a proposition for you."

Brody nearly choked. Had he stepped right into another messy situation? Granted, Mari was sweet, but the last thing he needed was to potentially ruin his relationship with a neighbor.

Tell your dick that.

True. He should be alone. Still, that didn't keep him from asking.

"What kind of proposal?" Intrigued, he followed her to the checkout counter. He only had a few of the items he'd planned on buying, but his curiosity was piqued and the rest could wait.

She bit her lip. It was adorable and sexy. "I need to work it out in my head first before I tell you. So come over for dinner in an hour and I'll explain. Bring your chips and salsa. I'm about to rock your world with some of the best tacos you've ever had."

She winked at him.

Everything about her was fun. He should lighten up. Besides he couldn't resist her offer without looking like a complete jerk. Not that he couldn't be a hard-ass, just ask the men and women he commanded. No doubt his face was used as target practice on dartboards all over the base.

"That's a pretty big claim. Tacos are one of my main food groups." It wasn't a lie. He had them three or four times a week.

"Ha! I'm a native Texan," she said with a slight twang that hadn't been there before. "If I can't make a great taco, they'll kick me out of here." Then she batted her eyelashes at him.

He laughed. It was a meal, what would it hurt? And they had helped each other out. She'd shown she was a good sport.

"All right. You're on." He wasn't sure he could recall the last time he'd smiled this much, and he was hungry.

As she headed to her car in her short shorts and football jersey, he put his items up on the checkout counter and smirked.

What he needed more than anything was peace and quiet, to focus on being a helicopter pilot and instructor. He'd been given a great opportunity for someone his age and he didn't want to screw it up by losing his drive.

That woman was trouble.

Damn if he didn't want to find out what kind.

What was I thinking?

Mari tossed her groceries into the fridge, which was in the garage. That's where she'd set up her temporary kitchen while hers was under construction. How was she going to cook a meal for a man like him on her tiny hot plate? And where exactly was she going to serve it?

She tapped a finger against her chin. The inside of her house was chaos. A construction zone with no end in sight. She sighed. She didn't have time to worry about that now. She had to plan dinner.

One hour at a time she reminded herself. It was how she lived her life now. Otherwise it was too overwhelming.

Inspiration hit. Her back deck. It was clean and she had a great fire pit to keep her and Brody warm. The hot tub hadn't been installed yet, but there was a decent table and chairs. She rolled her eyes; she wouldn't have used the hot tub with her to-die-for neighbor anyway.

Don't go there.

So handsome. So built. No. Not even a possibility. She needed him for one thing and one thing only—and it was not to satisfy her lust-fueled thoughts. Although feeling those manly muscles around her shoulders—and those abs.

Those abs. He must work out every stinkin' day. She shook her head as if to erase the image.

Nope. Not going there. She had a plan, or at least the beginnings of one, and it did not include having sex with the neighbor. No matter how terrific he might be.

No. Really. Stop thinking about him that way. Mere moments ago he'd had to extricate himself from the clutches of his boss's daughter. The last thing he wanted was Mari trying to seduce him. But it had been so long. So very long since she'd even felt the urge to—

Tacos. She had to get the tacos started.

She switched on the hot place, got out a frying pan and crumbled the hamburger meat into it. After adding some spices and a bit of minced garlic, she started chopping vegetables and shredding cheese.

This meal was the least she could do for her white knight of a neighbor. When he'd appeared out of nowhere and pretended to be her boyfriend, she'd almost collapsed with gratefulness.

The ex, Gary, had left a soul-crushing mark on her, and she wasn't sure she'd ever trust another man. He'd made her believe they had a future together, and then he'd come home one night and said she was boring. That he'd had an affair at a conference and it helped him realize he wasn't as into her as he thought he was.

Whatever. The cheating jerk acted like everything was her fault.

"You're too vanilla, Mari," Gary had said. "I'm not sure I've ever been this bored in bed. I shouldn't have cheated on you, but after that one night at the convention I knew what I was missing. And then I couldn't help myself. You're just not it for me."

Queasiness hit, as it did whenever she remembered his words. He could have shot her and left her for dead that day and she wouldn't have been more surprised.

It wasn't the first time a romance of hers had gone down in flames. She'd dated her fair share of Garys, but she'd thought this one was different. Even if their ideas on design clashed, and he didn't like Mexican food and he demanded the towels be folded in halves, when she liked them another way.

Who didn't go for a three-quarter fold? It always looked nice on the towel rack.

That should have been my first clue. Still, it didn't keep her ex's words from churning through her head in a hateful litany. All right, fine, so she wasn't an expert when it came to sex, and she'd had to fake the majority of her orgasms with Gary.

Oh, who am I kidding? I faked them all. But she didn't imagine she was boring in bed.

Now Gary was with a model? And she didn't even know what *bygones* meant. But she was probably great in bed, which evidently was Gary's primary criteria when it came to the woman he wanted to marry. Engaged. Already.

Ugh.

She rolled her shoulders, trying to ease the tension, and took a couple deep breaths. It's what she did to release the nerves.

I'm definitely better off without him. That fact didn't keep the loneliness at bay, however; and all the good guys in Corpus Christi seemed to be taken or unavailable. Even the hot, sexy Marine from across the street was too good to be true. He had women like the redhead throwing herself at him and there he was turning her down. How could Mari compete with that? Not to mention, what if she did sleep with him and he thought she was boring?

Why are you even thinking about sleeping with him?

Come on. How could she not? Those biceps and

that smile. When he'd thanked her ex at the grocery store for giving her up, her heart had skipped a beat. She had to remind herself *he was too good to be true*.

But it felt wonderful to have him in her corner. And that fish face Gary had made, that was the best.

No, it wouldn't do at all for her to think about Brody as anything more than a nice neighbor.

Although he might be able to assist her with the one thing she needed most.

She'd seen him in uniform a couple of times and he was breathtaking. After he'd carried in her flooring that day, she kept meaning to take him cookies or maybe bake him a pie. But without a real kitchen it wasn't easy.

She stirred the meat and then returned to chopping.

Her cell rang and she checked it. Mom again. She swiped the screen, making the phone silent. She didn't have time for this. And she knew it was only her parents checking in. They were still worried about her breakup with Gary even though it had been months ago.

Her ex's expression when he'd taken in Brody had been hilarious. As if the idea had never occurred to him that she could attract someone like the Marine.

Even if she couldn't, she sort of loved the fact that now Gary would think she'd traded up, silly or not.

Brody...he was all man. Those biceps under his black T-shirt could not be denied. And when she'd leaned against him, those abs she'd touched were washboard-hard. That was the third time she'd thought about his abs.

No. Do not go there.

Admittedly, in hindsight, the lack of sex between her and Gary hadn't helped their situation. It wasn't as if he had been initiating things and she was turning him down. They often came home tired. She was always busy with her interior design business and closing on the old Victorian, and he worked for one of the top architectural firms in South Texas. But she'd failed to see the signs. They had been going through the motions.

Still, it didn't mean he had a right to cheat. He'd met his fiancée at the convention and told her it had been love at first sight, and that he couldn't pretend any more with Mari.

Pretend.

She took another deep breath. The hurt still stabbed at her chest.

I'm over him.

I'm lucky he's out of my life.

Her brain believed her. Her heart, not so much.

Focus on dinner.

After digging around in her many boxes, she found the small red bowls that matched the plates she wanted to use. It was late January in Corpus Christi, which meant eating outside would be chilly, but fine with a fire. She took some wood from the cord she'd bought, then dashed through the house and stacked it in the fire pit out back.

Then she set the old wooden harvest table she'd stored there on the deck.

She opened the garage door to let out the smell from the meat that was cooking, and standing there was the dreamy Marine with a confused expression on his face.

Not expecting him to be standing there, she jumped and maybe screamed…a little.

"Sorry," he said. "I didn't mean to frighten you. Uh, why are you cooking in your garage?"

"Long story." Now she'd have to recount her very ugly history with this darn house. If he didn't already think her lame, he would soon.

Oh, well.

It's not like you wanted to make him yours.

Liar.

"Follow me and I'll explain everything."

2

BRODY FOLLOWED HIS neighbor through her house, which looked like a war zone, and after several tours in the desert, he'd been in a few. It wasn't junky, but most of the walls had been taken down to the studs. And the wood floor had large holes in it.

"Watch your step," she warned as she led him out to the backyard. "There were plumbing issues and they had to rip up some of the boards to find the pipes under the house. One of the five million things that have gone wrong since I bought this place."

The despair in her voice was clear. Why was someone like her living in this mess? He'd seen her in heels and brightly colored dresses when she came home at night. Even in her shorts and jersey she was immaculate. It didn't make any sense.

"I knew we, I mean *I*, was in for a lot of work, but I really underestimated the project. If I'd done this with one of my clients, I'd have been fired."

They stepped out onto a wooden deck. There was a table set with smart-looking ceramic bowls positioned near a fire pit. Strings of twinkling lights wrapped around the wood posts and portico. This was more of what he expected from Mari's house. It was casual but in an elegant sort of way.

"Clients?" he asked as he sat the chips and salsa on the table.

"I'm an interior designer. I have my own firm, but I work with architectural and construction companies around Corpus Christi and South Texas to design spaces from the ground up."

He didn't know anything about design, but he'd helped out at his uncle's construction company every summer in North Carolina. His family had moved a lot over the years, but the summers at his uncle's were something Brody looked forward to when school was out. Even though it was hard going, he'd enjoyed being a part of building homes, or at other times doing smaller remodeling jobs. From the look of her house, she had a hard road ahead of her.

"I can guess what you're thinking." She laughed. "I'm insane. You aren't wrong."

He laughed, too.

She glanced at the table. "I forgot the taco shells and sangria. Or would you rather have beer?"

"I'm good with water." Alcohol made the headaches worse and the headaches led to nightmares of his men screaming, waking him up in the early morning hours. The other night he'd left the ceiling fan on and he'd freaked out for a few seconds, imagining the blades from the Viper helicopter coming at him. Once he'd realized what was going on, he sent his fist through the bedroom wall.

Another patch job to add to his list of things to fix around the rental.

Most of the older homes in the neighborhood were stately and needed a lot of upkeep. His rental wasn't as big as Mari's, but it was just as old. Most of her Victorian had been remodeled, he noticed.

She frowned. "Oh, are you an, um— Sorry."

"No, I don't have a drinking problem. I *can* drink. But I want to lay off for a while. Been getting headaches and alcohol only seems to fuel them." Why was he telling her that? It would lead to more questions.

"Got it. Were you injured? Uh, I don't want to pry." Yep. More questions.

"Yes." He couldn't tell her. Couldn't talk to anyone about it. "My last tour we hit a bad patch." That was putting it mildly. But Brody refused to think about that flight.

She smiled and then touched his arm. It was a kind gesture. "Oh. Sorry I brought it up. Okay. Be right back."

He wished she'd just tell him what it was that she wanted to talk about. *Her proposal.* And he really hoped it wasn't to do with sex, although that's pretty much all he'd thought about for the last hour.

He didn't think he'd be able to tell her no, but it was the wrong choice for him right now.

"That's a lot to carry, I'll help."

"No problem. I got it. If you don't mind, maybe you could get the fire going?" She handed him a lighter from her pocket. "The temperature's good, but as the sun goes down it will get pretty cool out here."

"Sure." He should have suggested that they eat at his house, but he was worried about offending her. More than ever he was curious about whatever proposal she had. Strange that she'd invite him for a meal when she didn't have a proper kitchen. Not that he was one to judge. There were many times he'd used a hot plate, either in the barracks or at a temporary camp.

She emerged from the house with a pitcher of sangria in one hand and in the other hand she held a plate full of taco shells. She'd also tucked a bottle of water under one arm.

He grabbed the pitcher and the water and put them on the table.

"I had to heat the shells up in the microwave. Usually I'd do that in the oven, but I probably won't have one for another three weeks, and that's if the cabinetmaker finishes on time. His wife is having twins, so it's probably a little sad that I say nightly prayers she doesn't have those babies before he's done with my job. I'm a horrible person."

He laughed. "You're not horrible. You made me

tacos." He meant it. The meat smelled great and he couldn't wait to dig in.

She handed him a plate with four tacos on it. "My apologies again. Didn't mean to unload on you. It's been a *day*. You were there for part of it, but before that came the plumbing news."

She took the top off a large tray that had several small bowls. "I wasn't sure what you liked, so there is cheese, tomatoes, jalapeños and some caramelized onions. Oh, and I made guacamole. I left it in the fridge. I'll get it."

He loaded up his tacos and waited for her to return.

"This smells delicious. It's been a long time since someone made me an actual meal." Mostly he ate at a couple of local restaurants or the chow hall on base. The last six months he'd had to remind himself to eat. Food wasn't that important to him. The second he let his guard down, the guilt overtook him.

The muscles in his gut tightened.

No. He had to force the visions from his head. His men were gone. They'd never share another meal.

And this wasn't the time.

Focus. He had a beautiful woman sitting in front of him and she was sweet. He could try not being a hard-ass for an hour. And he was still more than a little curious about her proposition.

"Cooking is one of the things I do to relax,"

she said. "I miss it. I haven't had a kitchen for two months, well, one that had more than a hot plate in it. But enough about that. How did you end up here? What do you do?"

"I'm a helicopter pilot. I fly Vipers and Venoms, and when necessary, Stallions. I'm teaching Boots studying navigation at the base."

"Boots?"

"New Marines." His CO's order that he develop better camaraderie with the new squad flashed through his head. Brody didn't understand why he had to make friends. His job was to teach these guys how to best do their jobs so they didn't die. Maybe if he'd prepared his other squad more, they would have survived.

His gut tightened again, the wave of sadness culminating in the pain and tension behind his right eye. Why did it always seem that when you cared about people they ended up dead?

"Brody? Is something wrong with the taco?"

Blinking, he refocused. After taking a bite, the spices a perfect blend with the meat and toppings, he shook his head.

He pointed the taco at her. "You didn't lie. It's really good."

"Told you." She paused. "You don't sound like a Texan, in fact you don't have much of an accent at all."

"My dad is an entrepreneur and we moved a lot.

Sometimes two or three times a year. More after my mom died."

"Wow." Mari frowned. "That must have been hard on you as a kid. And I'm so sorry about your mom."

"It was and I do miss her. But it was a long time ago," Brody said. He still smiled when he thought of her. His mom had been the one to make all the moving seem like an adventure. "And to be honest, it taught me to travel light."

"Still, adjusting to new schools and stuff. And always making friends. I can't even imagine how difficult that must have been."

It was part of the reason he was such a loner. It was just easier that way. "So, Mari, can I ask why you decided to take on this house? Seems like a lot for one person."

She grimaced and put her food back on her plate. He'd upset her, but he didn't know how.

"True. It's a lot. But I didn't have a choice really. This started out as a project my ex and I had agreed on together. I bought the house and he would pay for the renovations, which were actually more than the house was worth. By the time we'd be finished though, the house would be worth four times as much. The plan was to flip it and move on to the next place. Except…the day after I closed on the house he broke up with me."

"Low blow," Brody said through gritted teeth.

"Not going to argue with you. And I can think of

some nastier things to say. Anyway, I was stuck. I can't sell the house as is, I won't get back the money I put into it. So my only option is to fix it up as best I can and sell. But without his money, I'm having to do it all on a shoestring."

Her ex deserved a load of bad karma for doing this to Mari. Brody hadn't known her long, but she was sweet, and didn't deserve to be treated like that.

Thinking of the situation at the grocery store only made him angrier. After all the jerk put her through, then he rubbed her nose in the fact he was marrying another woman.

"Do you need me to kill him?"

She smiled. "You know, earlier today when I found out how much it was going to take to bring the plumbing up to code, I might have taken you up on that. No, my proposition, well, it's a little out there."

"Just ask. Honestly, my curiosity is starting to get the better of me."

She sipped, more like chugged, the sangria. Then she set down her glass.

"I watched you fixing the roof on your house a couple of weeks ago. And then you repaired the mailbox and put in a new post. I promise I'm not stalking you, but I've also seen you tinkering with your motorcycle. A lot. And your truck. I just wondered if maybe you might be able to help me out around here. Maybe there's something I could do for you in return. Wait. That came out really wrong. I meant cook or something." She laughed nervously.

It took him a minute to figure out what she was proposing. "You'd like me to do handyman stuff?"

"Yes. Over the years I've learned a lot. I've even helped out on jobs. I have to bring in tradesmen for the electrical and plumbing, and those guys aren't cheap. So most of the other work is going to fall to me. This time, as I explained, I can't afford to hire the guys I normally would."

He pressed his lips together. It wasn't a matter of him not being able to do the work. He could. But hanging around Mari all the time probably wasn't a good idea.

She was the sexiest woman he'd met in, well... forever. And he didn't need complications like that. And he sure as hell didn't want to care about her or her rickety house.

He glanced up to see her chewing on her lip again.

"It was a dumb idea. Forget I asked. Really."

"No. It's that I'm pretty busy at the base. Lots of new recruits and..."

Liar. He could do the job in his sleep. And he was out of there every weekday at five because he didn't like being reminded of the past, which left him hours at home with nothing to do.

"Of course. Like I said, forget I asked. I don't know why I even thought it—I probably sound totally desperate. Can we just drop it? Please?" She cleared her throat and averted her eyes.

Shoot. He'd disappointed her. Her ex had left her in a bad spot, and Brody wasn't the kind of guy who could say no if someone genuinely needed his help. He'd done his best when he'd visited the families of his team members to make sure they got the benefits they were due and lend a hand any way he could. It didn't get rid of his survivor's guilt, but it made him feel useful. Mari was a kind woman who didn't deserve what life had thrown at her; he hated to see injustice of any kind, no matter what form it took.

"Tell you what, let me see what my schedule's going to be like the next couple of weeks. Maybe I can take care of a few things on the weekends, or some weeknights. Can I let you know tomorrow?"

Her head popped up and her smile did strange things to his insides, not to mention what was going on in his lower regions. He was glad she couldn't see under the old table.

"Are you sure? I mean, if you decide it's a no, I'm okay with that. You helped me more than enough today."

He had a feeling it was going to be hard to say no to Mari, and this was just the start.

THE NEXT MORNING at her Bay Area office bungalow, Mari crossed her arms on her desk and put her head down. This was why she was swearing off men.

"I'm an idiot."

"Hey, don't be so mean to my boss. She's a sweetheart."

Mari lifted her head as her trusted assistant, Abbott, walked in and took a seat on one of the upholstered chairs in front of her desk. She was also her closest friend. One of the few people Mari could confess to about her crazy night with the Marine. The one where she'd put the poor guy on the spot and begged him to fix her house.

What was I thinking?

"Still an idiot. You won't believe what I did yesterday."

Her friend steepled her fingers and waggled her eyebrows. "Oh, this has got to be good. I haven't seen you this bent out of shape since you broke up with the turd, which, let me remind you, was the best thing that ever happened to you. Do tell."

Abbott had been joyous over the breakup with Gary. She'd always disliked him. If only Mari had listened to her friend's warnings, she might have saved herself some heartbreak.

She told Abbott about what happened.

Her friend sat back and blew out a breath. Her brown curls in a righteous halo were piled on top of her head. "Wow! A true hero. What a great guy."

Mari lifted her face to the ceiling. "I know, right? And you should see his abs. He's hotter than any man has a right to be. That's what makes what I did next so atrocious."

Abbot's eyes widened. "You threw yourself at him? I told you this not dating thing was going to backfire on you. Those hormones can only be caged without release for so long. And then, boom!" She slapped the desk and made Mari jump.

Her friend had a thing for the dramatic. "No. Though, I wish I had. It's probably the last time I'm ever going to see him. He'll probably move."

Abbott leaned forward on her elbows. "Now I'm totally intrigued. Seriously, what did you do this time?"

"I asked him to be my handyman."

If she hadn't felt so bad she might have laughed at her friend's confusion.

"Is that some kind of new kink? I've never heard of that. Does he show up in just a tool belt or something?"

"Wow. Come on, Abbott, do you ever think of anything but sex?"

"Nope. Not really. So what do you mean?" Abbott wasn't supercrazy about commitment, either, but she also never lacked for a date. Her friend was the queen of love 'em and leave 'em. Mari had never been able to do that. Just have sex to have sex. In a way, she was envious of her friend's ability to have fun without getting emotionally attached. It wasn't that Mari was clingy. She just wanted something more than just the physical from her sexual partners. Not that it had worked out well for her so far.

She explained.

"Wow. You really are desperate."

Mari frowned. "Thanks for pointing out the obvious."

"So what did he say?"

"He was sweet. He said he'd think about it, but he added he was really busy at work."

"So he gave himself an out?" Abbott asked. "Hmm."

She nodded. Secretly, Mari had been a little crushed when Brody had said he was busy, which was stupid since she'd never believed he'd agree to her off-the-wall plan. "I think he was trying to get out of it gracefully, and he didn't want to have to tell me to my face that I was totally crazy."

Abbott leaned back. "So what are you going to do?"

"Well, I can't afford to move. Though, I did consider it. Living with my parents again, well, I just can't go there." She was only half-joking. Part of her wanted to give up on everything and go home to Austin. Her parents would understand. Heck, they'd probably welcome her with open arms. It'd been more than a year since she'd been to Austin to see them. She was always too busy with the *next* project.

Strangely, given everything that had happened, she wasn't sure she could handle being around them. Theirs was the standard to which she held all relationships—thirty years together and they were so in love with one another it was annoying.

Nope. She couldn't handle being around that right now.

There was also the fact that she'd built an up-and-coming business in Corpus, and she wouldn't give that up for any man. No matter how embarrassed she might be about her failed romance.

She'd have to stick it out and figure out how to hide from, or at least avoid, her oh-so-hot neighbor.

"So play it cool. Tell him you had too much sangria and it went to your head."

She pursed her lips. "That might work. Or I could simply barricade myself in my basement."

Her friend laughed. "Mari, we don't have basements in Corpus. How about I come help you paint one of the bathrooms this weekend?"

"You want to secretly stalk the Marine."

"True. But can you blame me? You make him sound so yummy. And he didn't take his tacos and run when you propositioned him with the worst offer ever, which means he's superbrave. Brave guys are so hot."

Mari shook her head. "Don't even go there. Though I might take you up on the offer to paint. That is if I can figure out how to get the drywall up. That stuff is heavy. I gave it a try in the dining room last night. By the fourth board I was in tears. I gave up and drank the rest of the sangria."

"Oh, you are so sad. You make my heart hurt. Incidentally, Mercury is in retrograde and it affects everyone in a negative way. However, it's going to get better. All of it. The house. The men. You're just in a downturn."

Mari didn't know anything about how the planets aligned, but she definitely could use a bit of luck. "That's pretty optimistic coming from you." Abbott called herself a pragmatist, yet Mari had always thought it bordered on pessimism. And it was weird that her practical friend had this fascination for horoscopes, as in she believed how the planets aligned ruled human emotions. More importantly she was a brilliant designer and an even better friend.

If only she could believe Abbott. That it would get better. But she'd been through two months of chaos and confusion, and while she wasn't one to feel sorry for herself, her perfectly ordered life was in the garbage. For the first time, she didn't have a plan, other than trying to get the house finished without ending up bankrupt.

The no security thing was a big deal for her. While her business was doing well, her stash of savings had dwindled quickly, thanks to her time-money-suck of a house.

It was a shame she'd royally screwed things up with the Marine. He was so caring. Guys normally didn't do what he'd done for her in the grocery store. But there was also pain in his eyes, and it wasn't due to the headaches he said he suffered from. Over the past few weeks, she'd noticed through her non-stalking observance of him that he pretty much kept to himself. If she wasn't such an idiot, they maybe could have at least been friends.

With benefits.

Stop it.

Well. Truth. No man had affected her physically like he did. She wasn't into casual sex, but he made her think all kinds of naughty things.

Really. Naughty. Things.

3

"CO WANTS TO see you in his office." Ben Peterson, one of the other instructors, popped his head into the classroom.

"What kind of mood is he in?" Brody asked, though he knew the answer.

Peterson rolled his eyes. "Let's say I may need a new ass by the time this assignment is over. I just got chewed out for failing to enlist my fellow blah, blah blah. He starts talking and I don't even hear what he's saying after the fifth or six word. Good luck."

Brody chuckled and then winced. He'd been grading tests and his head hurt. The last thing he needed was the CO on his back. He gathered his laptop and his phone and stuck everything in his pack. Might as well get it over with, and then he'd go for a run. Get rid of the tension of the day. His Boots weren't absorbing the test material like they should. The test scores were low. Somehow the CO saw that as his fault and not the problem of the undisciplined grunts under his command. The ones who spent a lot of time thinking they were on some sort of vacation rather than studying. Not that he had been much different when he was a grunt, but he'd quickly learned if you wanted to make it in the pilot or navigation programs, you had to be dedicated.

He rubbed the back of his neck as he strode through the long corridors. Seemed like the harder he tried with this job, the worse things were. Some days he wondered if he should just go ahead and get cleared for active duty again. Maybe he wasn't suited to be an instructor.

But first he had to lose the headaches. They were a distraction that interfered with his flying. He couldn't protect people if he had a blinding migraine.

He partly blamed Mari's proposal for the tension today. He'd been thinking about her a little too much. That sweet smile of hers and her ability to make such a great meal on a hot plate were turn-ons. The rockin' bod and beautiful eyes didn't hurt, either.

His body tensed.

Mind out of the gutter.

He had a new rule. One he'd added to his code in the middle of the night when he couldn't sleep. No more attachments. Ever. Life was easier like that.

Mari deserved the kind of man who could cherish and protect her. A man who could make that lifetime commitment and wanted the white picket fence.

That man is not me. Maybe he had a little of his father in him after all, because when it came to women, Brody couldn't see himself settling down. That might make him selfish, but at least he was aware of it—unlike his dad, who seemed to be perpetually married, perpetually looking.

He'd had a string of stepmothers, several he'd never met, since he was off serving in combat missions for the better part of the last ten years. Though his dad's recent email had mentioned he was single again, it wouldn't be long before his father hooked up with someone else.

Not my thing.

Nope. Women were a distraction that he didn't need right now. He liked his quiet life.

The outer office was empty, so he knocked on the CO's door.

"Enter."

Brody straightened his shoulders before he turned the knob.

"Sir, Peterson said you needed to see me."

The other man nodded, but didn't look up from the papers he was signing.

"My daughter tells me you have a girlfriend."

What? Aw, man. He remembered meeting up

with Carissa at the grocery store. "It's kind of new." That much was true. They'd only just met officially.

"Good to see you making friends. Be sure to bring her to the picnic on Saturday." What the...? The CO was ordering him to bring a date?

There's no way he'd drag Mari to anything base-related. That part of his life he wanted to keep private. Besides, the less time he spent with her, the better. The more he thought about her proposal, the more he thought it might be best to stay as far away as possible.

"She's pretty busy on the weekends renovating an old Victorian." Again it was the truth. "I'm not sure she'll be able to get away." He stood by the door, hoping that he could make a quick escape.

"It's only a few hours. You're in charge of a large squadron. We like to see our Marine instructors as leaders. Setting a good example. Are we clear?"

"Yes, sir."

Now he had to tell his CO the truth.

One of the support staff stuck his head in the door behind Brody. "Sir, your daughter is on line two."

The CO nodded. "You're dismissed, Brody." Then he picked up the phone.

Brody hesitated. He had to be honest about Mari, he owed it to her, if not himself, but the other man motioned him out.

What have I done? He couldn't ask Mari to a silly picnic. After his abrupt departure last night, she probably hated him. He'd finished his tacos, chugged his water and then booked it as fast as possible. He'd promised to think about her proposal and he had.

Bad idea.

But did he have a choice? She was a woman in need. Though he liked to think of himself as tough and unsentimental, he couldn't leave her in the lurch. The house was a disaster at the moment. It was sad that she had to live in it while she fixed it up. She should be in a fancy penthouse somewhere and enjoying her life.

Fine. He was going to help her.

And now he'd have to convince Mari to help him, as well.

Why couldn't people stay out of his personal life? That the CO thought it was better that his soldiers be married or engaged in order to get ahead made no sense to Brody.

But the CO hadn't really given him a choice. Toe the line or you're out. The message had been clear.

Forty-five minutes later, he was back home. He changed into his running gear and five miles after that he stood in front of Mari's door. Before he had a chance to knock, she opened the door. She must have seen him coming up the drive.

His shirt was stuck to him, and even though it was January, he was sweating from every pore. Probably should have showered first, but he didn't want to lose his nerve.

This had to be done. He had to at least try.

Her hair was in a high ponytail and she was wearing short overalls with a pink bikini top underneath. There was dirt on her nose, and he wasn't sure he'd ever seen anyone so gorgeous.

That bikini top was—

Eyes on her face, Marine. It was a challenge because of how she filled out the top, and then there was the curve of her hips. For the life of him, Brody couldn't look away. She was funny, gorgeous and good-hearted. And strong. To have gone through what she had with her ex, he had a lot of respect for her. He'd been thinking about that last night, too. Most people, men and women, would give up trying to fix something like this house on their own. But not Mari. He admired her work ethic.

And the idea of him lounging on his butt across the street while he knew she was struggling didn't sit well with him. They'd help each other out. Maybe even be friends. She might even cook him another meal.

She smiled.

Dang. Keeping his hands off her was going to be problem. But he had to do this. He was a Marine, trained to handle any situation.

"I'm sorry about last night," she said quietly.

"What do you mean?" Now that he thought about it, the night had been kind of perfect, eating tacos outdoors by the fire. Until he'd left like a jerk. She had no reason to apologize.

"Please don't make me repeat it. You know, the part about working on the house. We've just met and I feel dumb for asking you."

He'd made her feel bad. Now he really felt like a jerk.

"I will," he said quickly. "Help you, and I'll do it for free. But you have to do something for me in return. And it doesn't involve home-cooked meals."

She smiled. "Free? I'll do *anything.*"

His cock twitched, instantly ready for action. Was she flirting with him?

That loaded comment burned him from the inside out.

Be calm.

This would only work if they kept things casual between them. He didn't have many friends who were women, but he could do this.

He shifted to attention and put his hands behind his back to keep from touching her.

This might be tougher than he thought.

He cleared his throat. "I need you to be my girl-friend."

MARI WAS GLAD she had her hand on the door frame or she might have fallen to the dusty floor.

His girlfriend? This was some kind of weird dream. She'd fallen asleep while tiling or something.

Wake up, Mari! Wake up! You're probably snoozing on the bathroom floor.

Brody wore a tank that left his muscular biceps free. He must train for hours every day. The damp shirt clung to his abs.

Why am I so obsessed with this guy's stomach?

Because it's awesome.

What was he saying?

"Remember at the grocery store?"

"Not a day I will ever forget. You saved me," she said honestly. Her voice was slightly hoarse from the need coursing through her body.

Focus, Mari. Don't look at his... OMG. Eyes, focus on his gorgeous eyes.

"Right. Not that. After, when Carissa, my CO's daughter, came up. She told my boss we're dating and he's insisting we come to the picnic. I tried your excuse of 'we have to put in the floor' and had no luck. I even tried to tell him the truth about us, but he wouldn't listen."

Mari was still trying to adjust to the idea of the sweaty, broad-shouldered Marine being at her door. His muscles glistened. The man was too much.

Too much man for her.

"Picnic?"

"Yes." He ran a hand through his short, dark hair. He didn't have the buzz cut a lot of the Marines around town did. "I'm making a mess of this. Probably totally confusing you. See, they do these events where we all get together, something about creating a more cohesive unit."

"Okay? And you need a pretend girlfriend, why?

I mean, you're a good-looking guy, just about any woman would be happy to hang on your arm."

"You think I'm good-looking?"

She snorted. It wasn't very attractive.

He frowned as if he didn't believe her.

"Seriously? Dude, you're hot."

He looked skeptical. "I never really thought about it. Carissa saw us together and— Are you okay? You're all flushed."

Her entire body was warm from the top of her head to her toes. It had been a long time since she'd been this turned on. "Fine. I'm fine. So explain it again. Sorry, I'm a little out of sorts. I was working in the bathroom and then you showed up. And you want me to do this because…?"

His eyebrows drew together as if he was trying to determine if she was sane.

Right now, I'm not sure. Back away, handsome man. Back away.

"Anyway. I don't want a real girlfriend. I'm not good with that kind of long-term relationship. There are always too many expectations. And I…that is, I don't need complications right now. I need to focus on work and make sure my team is as strong as possible before they're deployed. So I was hoping that I could help you with your house, and maybe you could go as my 'friend' to these required outings the boss has put together." He air-quoted the friend bit.

She wasn't sure what to think. Why couldn't he form attachments? Do a long-term gig? Then again, she was in no shape for any kind of relationship, either. She was seriously off men for good.

No, for real. You are off men. No more. Ever. Well, at least until the house was finished.

And he's free labor.

And, oh, yes, she deserved a little man candy to look at. Every woman did. He could put up the drywall and she could stare at those powerful muscles of his.

There was that.

"What exactly would I have to do on these dates?"

He shrugged. "I don't know. Whatever women do. Can I be honest?"

"Sure."

"I'm up for a promotion. The CO wants to see that I'm settled. Stable. For some reason, having a woman in my life would make him think that I'll be more focused, which is not exactly how I see things, but he won't see reason. So, yeah. I just need you to act like you're into me, and be polite and stuff."

"All right, but so we're clear," she said, having a brief, rare moment of clarity. "I think this is a superbad idea. Someone will probably find out. And then we're both going to look foolish."

"Ten-four. I couldn't agree more. And if I could manage to tell him without him reading me the riot act for the fifth time this week, I would. But this will be more of a business relationship between us, right? You need a handyman and I need a girlfriend.

We fix up your place, go to a couple of events and chill out, and then we break up, like most couples do."

Hmm. "Can I be the one to break up with you?" She didn't know why, but that was a deal breaker.

He shrugged. "Fine by me."

"Can you tile a floor?"

"Yes."

"How good are you with a paintbrush?"

"Better than most."

"How about drywall?"

He peeked around her into the dining room behind her. "I could have those walls up in less than an hour."

Really? He would save her countless days and all she had to do was go out on a couple of dates with a good-looking guy?

And we're questioning this because…?

"Okay. I'll do it."

He smiled then, and her heart tugged. She suddenly remembered why this was a bad idea.

Danger. Danger. Danger.

"Really?" He stared at her as if he expected her to take it back or something. What? Were they in second grade?

Why not torture yourself? At least you get the eye candy up close. "Yes. It's a win-win. You'll be forcing me to get out of my house once in a while and I get free labor. I might even cook for you, as long as you don't mind simple food. I can't do much more than tacos on the hot plate."

He thumbed some dirt off her nose.

Great. So attractive. Should have washed her face or at least looked in a mirror before she opened the door. She'd caught a glimpse of him running up the street and had stood staring until he'd jarred her to her senses by approaching her house.

Well, at least she wouldn't have to worry about him making moves on her, given her messed-up appearance.

He was staring at her again as if she were crazy. Had he been saying something?

"Okay. Deal." She held out her hand and pretended to have been thinking about whether or not she wanted to do this.

His hand swallowed hers. It was so big and rough and she wondered how it would feel on—

"What are you working on?" he asked.

It took a few seconds for her to clue in to what he'd said. No sex. Just friends.

Keep telling yourself that.

"Bathroom fixtures arrived. I'm laying tile so I can put everything together."

"I can help you with that." He glanced down at his sweat-soaked shirt. "Forgot I might need a shower."

She shrugged, trying to act nonchalant. "Seems silly for you to get cleaned up only to get dirty again."

Dirty. Why did everything out of her mouth sound like sexual innuendo?

Because those shorts were tight against his—
Stop it.

She pushed away the idea of stripping that tank off him and running her hands across the tight abs underneath. Far, far away.

Until she was alone, later, in her bed.

He's staring again!

"Right. Tile." She opened the door wider.

"Cool." He stepped past her and into the house. "Is the bathroom on the second floor?"

"Yeah. First door on the right."

The man's backside as he climbed the stairs was a sight to behold.

Free labor. Free labor. Free labor.

No, this wouldn't be torture at all.

4

BRODY USED A rag to clean the last of the grout off the guest bathroom floor. The black-and-white hexagon tiles were dizzying up close, but when he stood and backed toward the door it made the bathroom appear bigger than it was.

"It's an optical illusion," Mari said from behind him. "And you did that so fast. I can't believe it."

"I put down floors in my grandmother's house the last time I was on leave. She wanted tile and wood, so I learned a lot through trial and error. Every summer from about the time I was eleven until I went into the Marines after high school, I worked for my uncle's construction company."

It was one of the final chances he'd had to be with his grandmother, and he was glad it was a happy memory. She'd died from complications from a stroke later that year. As her only grandson, and with his mom gone, his grandmother left him her house, which he'd sold. That place had nice memories for him, but the offer had been good. And it would be several more years before he'd be able to pick where he wanted to live. Probably not until he retired from the military. He missed her—she'd been the one constant in his life when he was growing up. Well, that and working with his dad's brother. But his grandmother had been such a solid female influence, and one of the kindest women he'd ever known. He rubbed his forehead and closed his eyes. Best not to start thinking about the past.

"I brought you some water, I didn't know you'd be done so fast." She handed him the bottle. Her pink bikini top was snug against her breasts and he had to force himself to look away. She was going to be his fake girlfriend, not the real one. It wouldn't pay for him to act on his attraction to her. Keeping it simple was how he made it through each day. Work, eat and sometimes sleep.

Her head cocked. She was watching him.

"So it needs to dry overnight, and then we can start moving in the cabinets and stuff. Is there anything else we should get done tonight?" He chugged down the water.

"You've done so much already, thank you." She handed him another bottle of water and took the empty from him. But her eyes were on the room behind him. He stepped around her, so she could have a better view.

"Wow. This is…wow. You really are fantastic at this. I mean, beggars can't be choosers and all of that, but I wasn't expecting it to look so professional. I'd hoped, but…this would have taken me at least a week and it wouldn't have been nearly as good. I feel like I should pay you."

"No," he said quickly. He really needed her to help with his CO problem. "I mean, we have a deal and I don't mind. To be honest, I like to stay busy." When you slept only an hour or two a night, it left a person with a lot of free time. His landlord had been so pleased with what he'd done to the house he was living in, she'd knocked another fifty bucks a month off his rent. He still wanted to do the landscaping for her, but that wasn't possible until spring.

"You didn't answer my question," he said.

She glanced back at him.

"About needing anything else done tonight?"

Her eyebrow rose, and he'd give anything to know what she was thinking. From the expression on her face, he wondered if she might have taken his question the wrong way. As in sexually.

Nope. He couldn't let his mind trip down that path, or he'd never survive the next week.

"There's always something to do around here, but it's almost nine. If you have time tomorrow night, maybe you could help me replace those fixtures. Meanwhile, the plumbing should be finished in the kitchen by Friday, until then I'm going to paint the bedrooms up here."

"I could paint one of the bedrooms tonight."

She put a hand on his arm. "You have to be exhausted. You worked all day. It can wait, and honestly, painting is the one thing I do fairly well. I'd rather use your help on some of the more difficult projects like the drywall." While still holding onto his arm with one hand, she reached back to point downstairs with the other. Her bikini top slipped just a bit. Her luscious tan globes were absolutely mouth-watering. A little farther and he'd see—

No. He forced himself to look away again.

That didn't keep her touch on his arm from sending heat to his groin. When he glanced at her hand on his forearm, she lifted it away as if he was hot to the touch.

"Sorry," she said. "I—I know some people don't like to be touched. I wasn't thinking."

He shrugged. "Not a big deal."

Except when you do it. What was that? The urge to pull her close and kiss her senseless was overwhelming.

Have to get out of here now.

"Okay. Right. It's late. You probably need your rest. I'll be back tomorrow to give you a hand," he said quickly. Then he was down the stairs and out the door before she could say anthing else. He hoped she hadn't seen the erection tenting his shorts.

Jerk. She probably thought he couldn't handle the soft touch of a woman.

You are a jerk and you can't handle her touch.

Her hand had been so fragile and small against his arm. What would it be like to feel her hands on his— If he had to spend time with her over the next several weeks, he couldn't let his thoughts get away from him. She needed a friend, not some sex-starved Marine who wanted in her bed more than he'd wanted anything in a really long time.

Damn. This was going to be difficult.

Friends. A means to an end. No way could he allow himself to think about her like that. She was too, too...

His front door slammed behind him. He'd been so preoccupied he hadn't realized he'd crossed the street.

That's what happened when you thought about women. They were a distraction. Definitely one he couldn't afford.

He stripped as he approached the shower, and a few seconds later he stood under the cold blast of water.

It didn't help.

His cock hardened and he wrapped his fist around it. He imagined it was Mari's small, delicate hand satisfying him, and wondered what it would be like to strip that bikini top off her and kiss those breasts. Even better, to suck and squeeze those beautiful globes.

He pounded the wall with his other hand. The marble rattled.

The next few weeks were going to be hell.

WHAT DO YOU wear to your fake boyfriend's work event?

Mari picked at the paint under her nails while

she stared at her closet full of clothes. No matter how hard she scrubbed, she could never quite get all the paint off her nails. And using turpentine at this point would only make her smell rank.

Brody had helped her paint the last of the upstairs bedrooms the night before. They'd also installed the new fixtures. The man was a champion. For the first time she'd been able to take a hot bath thanks to him replacing the hot water heater. She'd been showering in the closet-size downstairs bathroom, where the hot water only worked when it wanted to.

In the past few days—well, nights, really—he'd made her rambling money pit more of a home. When she'd showed him the plan she had devised on how to tackle the massive project, he'd given her a sweet smile. Then he'd revised it. What he'd come up with made a lot more sense. Maybe it was his Marine training, but he was extremely disciplined and organized. He put her to shame, but in a good way.

And once he started a job, he didn't finish until it was done. He was like a machine. He prioritized and completed the projects that had an immediate benefit to her, and it had made a world of difference to her life.

The toughest part was the ogling. She tried so hard not to stare at his muscles when he was on the job, but it was tough.

Really tough.

Who wouldn't stare? The man was an Adonis. Not a very chatty one, but he did like music. They agreed on most bands, which was surprising. Gary had hated her indie music. But not Brody. Every once in a while, his head would nod to the beat. Sexiest thing ever.

Who was she kidding? Everything about the guy was sexy.

That she hadn't kissed him yet was nothing less than a miracle. Every night he filled her dreams. But she refused to act on any of them. He'd made it clear, more than once, that she was just a good friend. And frankly, she needed every friend she could get. In fact, she'd done everything she could to make their time together as pleasurable...no, not pleasurable, as nice and relaxed as possible.

And today was her chance to show him how much she appreciated everything he'd done for her.

She picked up another top and held it in front of her.

Not this one.

This was exasperating. She had nothing to wear, and she hadn't had time to shop.

The new bath had been heavenly, but she'd stayed in too long and now Brody would be at her door any minute now.

When the sun was out, the temperature would reach seventy-five, but she didn't want to wear shorts. First, while her top half was somewhat tanned from working out in the backyard clearing out brush, her lower half was as white as white could be. And second, she hadn't shed the ten pounds she'd gained after her breakup with Gary.

Even with all the exercise while working on the house, those pounds of chocolate sea-salt caramels she'd eaten had added up. That was the main culprit responsible for the wardrobe problem she was currently having. A lot of her casual clothes were a bit tight. She found a pair of jeans and laid down on the bed to zip them up.

When she tried to sit up, they cut into her a bit.

Oh, well. I hear breathing is highly overrated.

"Hey, Mari, you ready? Where are you? Please tell me you aren't still painting the—" Brody paused. "I…oh, sorry."

Her hands flew to her not-so-covered breasts as he turned away.

The surprise on his face, and then the quick appreciation he'd shown, had her feeling a little better about her supertight jeans. Over the last few days she'd caught him checking her out as if he were interested, but he never tried anything.

Silly girl, you don't want him to try anything. At least she kept telling herself that.

No more men.

She had to get through repairing this house. Then selling it. And maybe after that she could think about dating again.

Maybe. Probably never.

Back to the situation at hand. He'd seen her half-naked.

That's not embarrassing at all.

"I didn't realize you'd moved into this room. I thought you were staying downstairs," Brody said as he trailed down the hallway.

"Since we finished the master bath," she called out, "I decided I'd just move up here." She found a bra and a vintage T-shirt. "And don't leave. Give me two seconds. I want to make sure you think I look all right."

Brody cleared his throat, but didn't say anything. She stepped into the hallway and spied him staring over the banister, looking down at the foyer.

"It's okay. I'm dressed," she said. "You can come back in."

He looked everywhere but at her.

"How is this outfit? It's a picnic, so casual, right? But do you think this is how the other women will dress?"

"You're beautiful," he said without ever laying eyes on her. He gazed up at the ceiling as if he was on the hunt for cracks in the plaster. There weren't any—he'd fixed them all. He'd put her new bed together a few hours ago, while she'd been downstairs making them sandwiches. Later, when she'd gone upstairs she'd found the bed made with clean sheets and the Pottery Barn comforter she'd bought.

It was those thoughtful things he did that made

her heart skip a beat. Even though she was trying her best to ignore it.

His hands were behind his back and he was still staring at the ceiling.

She laughed.

"They were just boobs, Brody. You can look at me now."

"They were very nice boobs," he said. His eyes narrowed and she had a feeling he was having a tough time looking at her. "You should be proud."

She laughed again. "I think there might be a compliment in there somewhere. I wasn't feeling so great about myself as I was getting dressed, so thank you."

His brow furrowed. "But you're incredible. How could you be down on yourself?"

She sucked in a breath, unable to breathe out. The man had no idea what those words meant to her.

He smiled a big, warm smile and she was momentarily distracted, stunned. Oh yes, he'd said something lovely.

"Thanks. So, I want to fit in, but I have no idea how people who usually wear uniforms think what's appropriate in an everyday situation."

He wore khaki shorts, a gray T-shirt that fit tight against his shoulders, and sneakers. He could have graced the cover of a fitness magazine. And he definitely did not have winter-white legs. As far as she could tell, most of him was a golden tan. She'd seen him running without his shirt a few times and wondered how many wrecks he'd caused from folks ogling him.

"I've never been to one of these events. I usually try to find an excuse to get out of it, but you look great. We should go. The last thing I need is the CO giving me a hard time about being late. The man lives to make my life difficult."

"Well, we can't let that happen." She realized she wanted to impress his CO. "But I still need to change my top one last time. I just thought of the perfect blouse to wear."

He turned and was almost downstairs before he said, "I'll meet you in the truck."

It had been a while since any man had taken notice of her, and she had to admit it felt good to have Brody's appreciation. She grabbed a frilly white top that had layers of lace and paired it with the jeans. It felt more beachy and feminine. And more than ever she wanted to look good on Brody's arm.

Even if all of this was fake.

Twenty minutes later they were pulling into the picnic area where the event was taking place. A large canopy had been set up with tables. There was beach volleyball and little kids were running all over the place.

She'd been so worried about getting ready, she hadn't thought about how she would interact with these people. There were a lot of families with teenagers and young kids—how would she relate?

"I'm nervous," she said. It was silly. She could

talk to most anyone. Part of her job as a designer was to convince her potential clients why she was the best person for the job. But that was her world, this was something very different.

Brody took her hand in his and squeezed it. "If it makes you feel better, I am, too. I live by a code and I don't like the idea of lying to my CO. But I keep telling myself it's worth it if it means avoiding Carissa. She's not a bad person or anything, but getting tangled up with her is the kiss of death. The last guy who had my job dated her for two weeks and then dumped her. I'm not sure where he was transferred to in the end."

"She's a grown woman, surely your CO wouldn't do something as vindictive as that?"

"He's tough about most things, which is why I don't understand all this pretend goodwill. You bond when you're deployed and when you're training, you're training. Like I said, I just don't get it. When I was a fresh recruit, I had to make it on my own. You have to be able to think clearly and rely on yourself. Sure, you always have your platoon's back when you're out in the field, but not like this."

"I've never done what you do, but I have had my share of bad bosses, or tough ones. And the truth is, you and I *are* friends. So, technically you aren't lying. You're still within your code. And you got me out of the house on a weekend, which has to be some kind of public service. If not for you I'd be bent over a paint bucket, or worse, dealing with the floorboards." She squeezed his hand and tried to ignore the heat sizzling through her body from his touch.

"I can't believe I had to rook you into this because of clingy Carissa."

"I'm doing you one favor; you've been there for me all week, Brody. And in a way that no one else I know has. You've quickly become one of my greatest friends, and not because you've worked so hard on the Victorian, but because you care. Trust me, it matters. But tell me the truth. Would you rather be with Carissa right now, or at my house helping me?"

"Hanging with you is definitely more fun."

That pleased her, probably a little more than she should have.

5

MARI TOOK A deep breath and stared out the windshield at all the people milling around the picnic area. She and Brody were in this together she reminded herself. "Let's do this! The faster we get out there, the sooner we can get back to the house and get those floors down in the kitchen."

He laughed. "You do have a one-track mind."

"Hey," she said as he got out and opened her car door. "I'll be able to cook real dinners for you once the kitchen is in place."

He held a hand out to assist her from the vehicle. "I like the dinners you make on the hot plate. I can't imagine how good the food will be in a real kitchen."

She smiled. He was so sweet. She'd made him stew the other night in the Crock-Pot and he'd talked about it for an hour. The guy really needed some decent meals. As for her ex, she couldn't remember a single time he'd thanked her for putting a meal on the table, even though she'd done so every night and they both worked long hours. But Brody was super-thankful, even if she presented him with nothing more than a sandwich.

"Brody, I'm glad you made it." The CO's daughter stood in front of his truck. Mari recalled her right away from the grocery store.

She snuck up on us. I wonder what she heard.

Carissa wore a white shirt tied at the waist and skinny jeans with heels. Mari had no idea how she walked on the sand in those things.

"Hey, Carissa, you remember my girlfriend, Mari," Brody said quickly. He leaned down and kissed Mari's cheek. Heat from his lips sent tingles through her body.

Down, girl. Down. She had to be careful or Brody would have to get a fake girlfriend to keep her away.

Mari waved at Carissa.

"Oh, almost forgot the potato salad," Brody said. "This is Mari's special recipe. I almost didn't bring it so that I could have it all for myself."

He grabbed the big bowl. She'd made the potato salad the night before, boiling the potatoes on the hot plate, which had been an experience since the pot she used was twice the size of the small burner. The recipe was actually her mom's and it always tasted better after sitting in the fridge for twenty-four hours. She'd had Brody taste-test it, and then she'd had to send him home before he ate the whole bowl.

"I had to hide it from him," she said truthfully.

"Um, okay then." The other woman didn't seem pleased or impressed with their closeness.

Whatever. Maybe her little scam with Brody was working and the other woman was finally getting the message. As in, back off. Even though Brody wasn't hers.

You need to keep reminding yourself of that.

"Food goes on the long table under the tent. Dad was looking for you," Carissa said, gesturing them toward the big tent. "He's out where they set up the croquet court." Then she swished away with what Mari thought was quite an exaggerated sway of her hips.

At the mention of the CO, Brody's shoulders had stiffened.

Poor guy. If the CO was anything like his daughter, Mari didn't blame him for being wary.

"It's okay," Mari whispered. And she took the bowl from him. "I'll go and set this down. You find your boss and I'll meet you out there."

"Nah. He probably wants to meet you. We'll go out there together."

"Big, bad Brody, are you scared?" she teased.

"Nope. I have you by my side, I can do anything."

He sounded so sincere. She almost tripped on her flip-flops as they headed toward the tent.

She deposited the potato salad on a large buffet table, uncovered the bowl and went with Brody to find his boss.

Brody put his arm around her as they neared a group of people standing by the edge of the water. It was a sunny day on the gulf, but the ocean would likely be cool given the time of year. The temperature had been cooler for sure.

Maybe I should have brought a sweater. Brody's warmth from his arm around her helped. She grinned.

"Sir," Brody said as they approached the group.

"Hello, Lieutenant. Introduce me to your friend."

"Yes, sir. This is Mari McDaniels. Mari, this is Commander Gray."

"It's nice to meet you, sir. Brody's told me so much about you." She held out her hand to shake his.

"I wonder if any of it was good," the CO said. His eyebrow cocked.

She laughed. "Always. He talks very highly about all the people he works with, though I have to admit I'm terrible with names. And even worse at remembering ranks and things. So if I say something wrong today, please don't see it as a sign of disrespect. Brody's doing his best to teach me."

She wasn't sure why, but she hadn't imagined Commander Gray would be so young or distinguished, especially since his daughter was in her early twenties. He couldn't be more than thirty-five, maybe forty, and that would be pushing it.

"Nice to meet you, Mari. You can call me Brenton. Are you trying to calculate how old I am?"

"I was thinking more along the lines of asking you to share your skin-care secrets."

The men around them chuckled, as did the CO. "Love a woman with a sense of humor," he said as he let go of her hand. "Carissa is my adopted daughter. When my sister and her husband were involved in a fatal car accident, I took responsibility for her. And, well, the rest is a long story for another day." Pain flitted across his face before he forced another smile.

"That explains it. I didn't mean to pry."

"No worse than the twenty questions you're going to get today," he said. "This is the first time Brody has brought someone special to one of our events. I have a feeling everyone is going to be curious."

Mari hoped they weren't too curious. She and Brody had only known each other a short while. If folks were too probing about what she knew about his past, she was sunk. And vice versa.

Whenever she and Brody were alone they talked about everyday things like movies, music and food. And they spent an inordinate amount of time discussing paint colors and what size moldings should go upstairs versus downstairs. They never talked about anything personal. After that one night over tacos, when he'd gone silent after she'd asked about why he couldn't drink, she'd shied away from asking him about private stuff.

"I won't lie. It's a bit overwhelming meeting everyone at once, but it's great to put faces to the names."

"So Brody's been talking about us?" the CO commented.

She shrugged. "I don't think you Marines talk much about anything." The guys around her chuckled some more. "And I'm afraid when we're together we're usually discussing what to do next with my money pit of a house." Sticking with the truth would make them seem genuine. She put an arm around Brody's waist and hugged him tight. "I don't know what I'd do without him. Hardest working man I've ever met."

Brody's arm squeezed her and he kissed her hair. For a fake relationship, everything felt amazingly real.

"So, Brody didn't tell us, what is it that you do?" the CO asked.

"Interior designer," she replied. "I have private clients, but I also work with builders in the area to help design the interior features of their homes. It's creative and fun, and that's what always appealed to me about it."

"Interesting," Commander Gray said. She was pretty sure he was merely being polite. She wasn't offended. These men and women dealt in life-and-death terms every day on the job. "I'm a big fan of older homes, they usually have more character, whereas Carissa likes anything new."

"Mari's a great decorator, but she's also very involved in preservation," Brody said. "You should see what she's doing with her house. She calls it the money pit, and maybe it is, but it's going to be a showplace when she's done. And she's sticking close to its historical details." He sounded so proud, but she was more impressed that he'd been paying attention.

"Like I said, he's been the hardest worker ever. I'm lucky to have him."

"I'd say he's pretty lucky to have you." The CO smiled. He seemed so nice, not at all the gruff old guy Brody had been describing to her. But then she knew that some people could have two faces. The one they used when in private, and the other when in public. She realized her ex had been that way. "And you finally got him to one of our outings. He's going to make a great leader some day."

Awww. See. He is nice.

Brody frowned as if he couldn't believe what the man had just said. Didn't Brody know what a great guy he was? Then she remembered what Brody told her about the CO always giving him a hard time. Maybe it was because he was grooming Brody for something bigger. Maybe the team-building stuff was more about him showing his potential as a leader. That would explain a lot.

"Well, on that, you and I can agree. I thought I was organized and efficient until I met him. You Marines really are the whole package."

"You've got a good one there, Marine. Take care of her."

"Yes, sir. I do," Brody said and he again squeezed Mari to him.

"Looks like the grub is ready," one of the men said.

Thank goodness. Saved by hungry Marines. She was afraid if the conversation went on too long she might say something that'd give her and Brody away.

"Let's eat," the CO said.

Mari was glad for the interruption, but she wasn't sure she'd be able to eat anything. Brody wasn't the only one who was nervous.

He held her back as the others headed for the tent. "Thank you," he said in a low whisper. "He actually paid me a compliment. I don't think that's ever happened."

She winked at him. "I bet he was trying to be a wingman of sorts. Trying to help me see you are a great guy."

"The CO as a wingman. That's funny."

"I know, right? As if you'd need help getting a woman. You probably have women propositioning you all the time. Since you needed me to chase them off, that says a lot." She meant it as a joke, but he didn't look happy.

"I'm not some womanizer. It's important to me that you know that. It's also true that I don't do committed relationships, but I don't sleep with every woman I meet."

Okay, she wasn't really sure where he was going with that. Why would he care what she thought of him? "It's fine." She lowered her voice. "It's not really any of my business who you…uh. Yeah. You know what? I'm really hungry. Let's go grab some barbeque."

Maybe they were better off not discussing anything too personal. When he'd mentioned other women her stomach had twisted and knotted. Thinking about him with other women wasn't her idea of fun. Still, it shouldn't matter, she reminded herself. Why did she have such a problem with his love life? They were just friends. Um. Friends who occasionally ogled one another.

No big deal.

6

BRODY FILLED HIS plate with barbeque, beans and tons of potato salad, and guided Mari to one of the picnic tables positioned under some shade. She'd held her own with the CO. He'd never seen the man smile or laugh like that. Mari had made him do both. She'd even coerced a kind word from him. That had never happened. Leader, my ass.

Unexpectedly, it had really bothered him that she thought he was the kind of guy who was only interested in one thing from women. True, when he'd come back from the last tour, he might have drunk more than he should have and gone home with more women than he should have, but that had only lasted a few months. When he became the senior instructor on base, he'd cleaned up his act…and fast.

That and he'd discovered the alcohol was contributing to his headaches. It seemed that nothing could make him forget what had happened at the end of that last tour.

Here he was alive and his friends were dead. He was thankful he'd caught on fairly quickly that drinking and carousing were not the answers. In their place, hard work and exercise had become his new demons of choice.

Except, he admitted, when he was with Mari. The hours he passed when he was with her went by so fast, he found himself disappointed each night when it was time for him to go home.

She was right, it shouldn't matter what she thought of him, but it did. In the last week, they'd become real friends. Good friends, in fact. And he'd been honest with her in the truck. He would rather spend time with her than anyone else.

He and Mari sat across from one of the men in his unit and his family. Mark had a toddler, a boy, sitting on his knee, and his wife held a baby girl. At least Brody thought it was a girl—the kid had a bow in the little bit of hair on her head.

"Your children are lovely. And so well behaved," Mari said as she and Brody got set to eat. "How old are they?"

Brody had been wondering the same thing. He took a bite of his barbeque.

"Thank you," Mark's wife laughed. "Most days I feel grateful if we all get out of the house dressed and with shoes on."

"I can't even imagine what it must be like with

little ones. I can barely take care of myself most days. By the way, I'm Mari."

"I'm Leslie, that's my husband, Mark. He's holding Jacob, who is eighteen months, and this is Lily. She is four months old and doesn't understand why she can't have my brisket."

They all laughed.

"I don't know who brought this potato salad, but it's made with mustard. I tried to take almost all of it, but Leslie wouldn't let me," Mark said.

"My Mari made it," Brody said proudly.

My Mari? What the—? That had slipped out. But he'd meant it. He was proud to have her with him today.

She smiled up at him. Each time she looked at him, this whole thing became less fake. If he was the commitment type, and he wasn't, but if he was, he would definitely be into her. But he had to remember that this was only an act. They could be friends but nothing more. He wouldn't want to hurt her, not after what she'd been through with her ex. Protecting her meant not sleeping with her. No matter how much he might want to.

The baby started crying. "Lily, why do you always wait until I'm ready to eat to start fussing? I just fed and changed you."

"I'll take her." Brody reached across the table.

Mari and Leslie looked at him as if he had two heads.

"What? I'm good with babies. Had lots of practice with my stepsiblings." After his mother died, Brody's dad had married four times. He had three stepbrothers and two stepsisters. As the oldest, and the one usually left in charge, he had changed more than his fair share of diapers. He'd left for the Marines at eighteen so he could get away from being a full-time nanny for his dad and stepmom number four, or was it five? He could never remember.

"I'm not going to turn down an offer, but she's picky about people. Don't get upset if she wails even louder."

Brody took the baby from Leslie's arms and then rested Lily against his chest. She was big enough that she could lift her head up and look at him.

He smiled down at her. "Hello, pretty Lily. I'm going to keep you company so your mom can get some grub. You gotta let her keep up her strength so she can take care of you. Then she can help you grow up and be big and strong."

The baby made a soft noise and then cooed at him.

"Wow. You do have the magic touch," Leslie said.

"She's probably afraid to piss him off," Mark cut in. "He scares the crap out of even the toughest guys in our unit."

He did? While Brody wanted the unit's respect, he didn't want anyone to be afraid of him. Did they look at him the way he did the CO? Hell. It never dawned on him that maybe he was just as gruff.

This day was full of surprises.

He'd always thought he was fair, but he did like to keep to himself. Maybe the CO was on to something with this bonding idea.

Maybe Brody should pay more attention to how he talked to the men and women in his classes. Maybe his need to stay separate from everyone was giving them the wrong idea about him. And if he wanted to be promoted, well, he'd have to show the CO that he wasn't just good at his job, but great with people.

Brody sighed.

He patted the baby on the back.

"Is that true? You guys are afraid of him?" Mari asked. "He's the biggest teddy bear of a man I ever met."

Mark gave a wry smile. "You've never failed one of his tests. He has a way of making you feel like you're two inches tall."

Brody's eyebrow lifted. He'd done nothing more than try to instill in them the need to understand the importance of navigation. Instruments went down, there could be air and ground assaults, a Marine pilot had to be ready for anything. That was why it was important for his team to study hard and make the grade. Their lives depended on it.

"Don't get me wrong, sir. We're a bunch of dumb..." he whispered and glanced down at his boy, "uh, jerks for not picking it up or studying hard enough. But you can be intimidating sometimes."

Intimidating? He never yelled. But maybe his silence was just as bad.

"How so?" he asked the other Marine. "I don't think I've ever said two words to you."

Mark smiled. "Yes, sir. But it's that look you give us sometimes. Scary as heck."

The baby burped loud and they all laughed. "Look at my big scary Marine," Mari said as she nudged his shoulder.

"I don't understand what these people are talking about, I'm the nicest guy I know," he said to baby Lily. She burped again loudly. "Right. I knew you'd understand."

Everyone around them laughed again.

"Man, who knew you were the baby whisperer," Mark said.

Brody shrugged. "Like I said, I had a lot of practice when I was younger."

Mari glanced up at him, and there was a question in her eyes. They never talked about their families or their pasts. He wondered if she had siblings. Her mom and her dad seemed to call her a lot, but she usually put her phone on silent. That seemed weird because he remembered her mentioning once that her parents had an enviable relationship. She'd also said she'd given up on finding the same thing.

That was wrong. She was entitled to every ounce of happiness she could get. But not with him. However, there had to be a nice guy out there for her. Although, the more he thought about it, the less he liked the idea. This thing with Mari was meant to be temporary and it wouldn't do to get too attached to her. Maybe he could find her a nice guy once they finished helping one another.

Again, the idea didn't sit too well with him.

They continued chatting with Mark and Leslie until the CO stopped by their table.

"Time for volleyball. Lieutenant, you're with me," the CO ordered as he pointed to him.

"Yes, sir." Brody nodded. Normally, he liked any kind of physical activity, but he wasn't looking forward to this game.

"You going to be my good luck charm?" he asked Mari. He handed the baby back to her mother and then gathered their trash.

"Aren't I always?" she joked. She followed him as he dumped their plates and they headed out to the beach, where the net had been set up.

Why had the CO asked him to be on his team? That was a lot of pressure. He frowned and rubbed the bridge of his nose. This was no time for a dumb headache.

"Hey," she said, grabbing his arm, "It's a game. Only a game. And he asked you to be on his team."

"That's worse," he muttered. His palms were sweating. "If I screw up, I'll never hear the end of it. You don't get it. He's nice to you, but every day he gives me grief. Every single day."

"Poor guy. Sounds like someone else I know. That's one of the reasons I decided to start my own business. In the beginning, being my own boss was a challenge. I hadn't thought about the fact that while I didn't have someone telling me what to do, I did have to deal with clients. But I learned to be a team player. There are better ways to approach things that won't make anyone feel threatened. From experience I know you guys don't like to be wrong."

"And you do?" He flipped his shades to the top of his head and rolled his eyes to take the bite out of his words.

That might work for her interior design business, but being a Marine was a little different.

"Listen, no boyfriend of mine is going to suck at volleyball," she said. Then she took his hand in hers and turned his palms-up. She traced the lines there.

Her touch instantly made him hard. How would he be able to focus now?

"Play for *me*. Don't think about anything else, except this." She kissed his palm. "Every time you score or set up a shot, I'll blow you a kiss."

A slow smile spread across his face. "And what happens if I win?"

She waggled her eyebrows. "If your team wins, I have all kinds of surprises for you," she said suggestively.

He barked out a laugh. "Well, when you say it like that." He turned her hand in his and then kissed her fingers. "Thanks."

He ran onto the sand to start the game.

When he glanced back at her, she blew him a kiss. Damn. He had to remind himself for the hundredth time that day that this wasn't real. But her affect on him was.

"Ready to play, Marine?" the CO asked.

"Yes, sir." He glanced over at her one more time and she winked at him. "I believe I am."

MARI'S FINGERS TINGLED from his lips.

Better be careful. This is also a game.

Just before he was ready to serve, he held up a hand. He ripped off his T-shirt, then ran over and handed it to her.

"Thanks, babe." He kissed her lightly on the lips. He might as well have stripped her naked on the beach given her body's reaction to him. From her head to her toes, she was a hot, needy mess.

She'd seen his muscles under the tanks and T-shirts he sometimes wore, but it was very different seeing them up close and personal.

It's just for show. It's just for show.

"How do you keep your hands off him when he does that?" Carissa asked from beside her. The other woman wasn't being catty, it was definitely admiration Mari heard in her voice.

She glanced around to find that she wasn't the only one with eyes on Brody. Though there were a lot of other very fit Marines playing the game, many sets of eyes were on Brody. She couldn't blame them—he was magnificent. "It isn't easy," Mari said truthfully. "But I've promised him, since this was a work event, that I'd behave. He said your dad doesn't appreciate PDA." At least, she hoped that was true.

"My *Dad*. Is really my uncle, and he's always a grump," Carissa sighed. "But he means well—most of the time."

Mari laughed. Carissa was probably one of the few people around the CO who could get away with saying something like that. But she wasn't super-crazy about her eyeing Brody. True, he wasn't really hers, but they didn't know that. And it was wrong for her to be drooling over another girl's man.

"If I were you, I wouldn't be able to keep my hands off Brody. By the way, how did you guys meet?"

"I don't mind saving it for when we get home. I like to keep him happy," Mari said, as if she meant it. "And he lives across the street." Once again she was sticking as close to the truth as she could. "It was one of those weird moments where he ran over to help me with some stuff in my car, and then... boom. Instant chemistry. Like I told you at the grocery store, I'd recently been through a bad breakup, so I was in no rush. But well, look at him. How could I ever say no to that?" Maybe that would get her off Brody's back. Poor guy. No wonder he'd panicked when he met her while shopping.

Brody helped set up a play and they scored a

point. He turned to look at her and she remembered to blow him a kiss. He pretended to catch it.

Cheesy. Yes. But it didn't keep the flutters from taking flight low in her belly.

That's dangerous.

I'm acting. Yep. Right.

And now she was talking to herself.

Speaking of bodies, that man's abs were outstanding. The last several mornings, as she'd been getting her morning coffee, she'd hear dogs barking in the neighborhood. The barking usually meant Brody was coming back from one of his twice-daily runs. She'd *accidentally* find herself at the front window watching his glistening body as he came up the street.

And he had to do weights to have all of those rippling muscles. What would it feel like to run her hands down—

"Whoa," the crowd around the game roared. Brody was in midspike. The other team didn't have a chance. The CO high-fived him. He glanced at her again and opened his hands as if to say "where's my kiss?" She smiled and blew him another one.

How he looked at her sent her body into a full-on heated flush. A potent combination of adrenaline and arousal sped through her veins. It had been a really long time since she'd had sex. Her ex thinking she was terrible in bed was the sort of comment that stuck with a girl. Whereas Brody made her dream about doing naughty things that would feel *so* good.

Maybe he could teach her—

No. Bad idea. First, he was free labor. And if she was really as terrible in bed as her ex said, then it would be all awkward and just plain wrong.

Probably best to keep Brody as a friend only.

The crowd roared again and she caught a glimpse of him as he high-fived the CO. Then he turned and winked at her.

She blew him another kiss.

He put a hand over his heart and the women around her sighed. Dang. He was getting into this. And so was she.

The rest of the game went by in a blur, as she imagined rolling around in the sand with Brody. Naked.

Wrong. So wrong. You can't think of him like that.

"Hey." Brody pulled her out of her reverie. "We won. And you owe me at least four more kisses." He glanced around them. "I'll make you pay up when we get home."

"That sounds like a threat." Her voice was low and raspy. "One I'm perfectly willing to give in on." And then she smiled at him. "You were kind of awesome out there."

"It was all for you, babe. You made this a great day." When he leaned down and kissed her lightly on the lips, someone walked past them and whistled. Brody leaned away and gave her one of his devastating smiles.

He had the towel from the beach bag and he was wiping the sweat from his arms and stomach.

Save me. Universe. Please.

"Can you get my back?" He handed her the towel and then turned around. There were scars up and down his spine. Some were round, others were thin and long, as if he'd been cut by something. While the round marks were faded, older perhaps, the slashes were pink and puckered, as if recent.

What had happened to him? He'd mentioned he didn't sleep much and there was always that hint of something sad in his eyes. The only time she'd seen it disappear was when he'd been talking to baby Lily.

She patted him down and then handed him the towel.

"Good game, Lieutenant," the CO said as he passed by.

"You, too, sir." Brody watched the other man with a smile on his face.

"Look at you, big winner. I bet you're happy," she said.

"I am. That was fun."

She laughed. "Yes, because you guys won."

"I'm surprised you noticed. You seemed kind of lost in thought while I was out there."

"I was thinking about the paint color for the kitchen. Maybe the off-white would be better. But then I worry about the whole thing being too white."

Liar. Big fat liar.

"I thought you'd settled on the cornflower blue," he said, as he took his T-shirt from her and slipped it over his head. She was sad to see the abs go, but it made it easier to focus.

"Too country for the Victorian. I'm thinking I need to stay true to the colors of the time period." *Good cover.*

"Hmm. It's up to you. I'm not a fan of the green that was in the bunch of historical swatches you brought home. And yellow always seems kind of girly to me."

She shrugged. Strange that they could have this conversation when a few seconds ago she was thinking about rolling around naked in the sand with him. "Yep. You're probably right."

"The blues seemed more calming," he said seriously. "I mean…it's your kitchen, you can do whatever you want."

"No, I like having a guy's opinion. The house has to appeal to all buyers. I appreciate the input."

"Hey," Brody said. "Before we head home, I was wondering if you wanted to take a walk on the beach. Mark was telling me about a bunch of starfish that washed up after the storm last night. They're trying to find volunteers to put the live ones back in the water a half mile down the shore."

"Oh, no. Patrick's in trouble," she said in her best SpongeBob impression, which was really awful.

He frowned. "Who is Patrick?"

He didn't get her joke. She laughed. "You know,

the dude who is the best friend of the guy who lives in a pineapple under the sea?"

He felt her forehead as if she had a fever. "Did you maybe get too much sun?" She batted his hand away.

"Silly. It's a television show. Patrick is a starfish and he's SpongeBob SquarePants's best friend. It's been on a while."

"I pretty much watch sports and news," he said.

"Borrring."

"So we'll go save some Patricks?" He held out his hand, and she placed hers in it and tried not to think about what the warmth of his touch did to her body.

It's all for show. It's all for show.

Yep. You keep telling yourself that.

7

BRODY SAWED THE boards he needed for the kitchen floor, trying his best to avoid looking at Mari. She was bent over another board measuring his cuts for him. Her cute shorts rode high on her creamy thighs, and he didn't even want to think about how his hand would feel on her ass.

No. Just no.

Ever since this afternoon at the beach, there had been something between them. But for the past several days, he realized they'd been getting to know one another—swapping stories, exchanging knowing looks. Even finishing each other's sentences. There was an innate calmness to her, almost soothing to him in a way. She was a balm to his dark soul, seeing the light in most everything. When things went wrong with the house, she'd roll up her sleeves and do whatever needed to be done. And she never complained.

He respected the hell out of her, which was the main reason he could never touch her.

Yesterday he'd been in a bad mood at the base and he couldn't figure it out until it occurred to him that he was missing her.

It was strange. He'd never been so attached or attracted to a woman.

And he couldn't tell her. One of the greatest temptations of his life, and there was nothing he could do about it. At this point, and it had only been a week, it was more about losing her as a friend, rather than a fake girlfriend.

Except it wasn't so fake anymore. She was the kind of woman he needed in his life, but temporarily. And she didn't need that.

She hummed and he paused to watch her again.

Her long hair was piled on top of her head and for the past hour he'd been consumed with the idea of taking it down and letting it fall to her shoulders. Then he'd capture her lips and…

"Brody? Are you okay?" Mari stood in front of him with a board in her hand.

"Yep."

She smiled and his cock twitched.

"What were you thinking about?"

"You," he said before he could stop himself.

What are you doing? Screwing everything up.

She blinked. "Me?" she asked as she set the board she'd been measuring on the sawhorse.

"Yes. It happens a lot, especially lately. You're

a gorgeous woman and I can't stop myself. It's a bad idea. I get it, as well as I know how to breathe."

"We— I mean, I think about you, too, but—"

His body tensed. She thought about him?

"It complicates things," he said, wondering if her thoughts were heading in the same direction that his were. "We're friends. Anything else will, like I said, be complicated."

She nodded.

He caressed her cheek with the back of his fingers and she leaned into his hand.

"Mari?"

"Yes." Her eyes were caught in the same web, neither of them able to look away.

"I need to kiss you."

"Yes. You should do that," she said as she took a step closer. "Friends kiss, right? I mean, they do it. Oh. Uh. Not what I meant. There's a whole movie about friends with benefits. Oh. Crap. I can't shut up."

He caressed her jawline with his fingers. "We can't do this. It will ruin everything."

"You're right."

She stepped so close to him, their bodies touched. Her breasts, the ones he'd been dreaming of, were pressed into his chest. A man could only take so much.

"But if we gave in to the sexual tension," she continued, "kissed and got over it, maybe we could move on. Be friends. We're probably making more of this than there really is."

She made way too much sense. But maybe the reality wouldn't match the fantasy?

"We're in agreement that this is a really bad idea."

"Stupendously bad," she said.

"Stupendously?"

"New vocabulary app on my phone. I'm trying to use a new word at least five times a day."

Wow, she was too much. But that didn't stop his lips from capturing hers.

Sweet. Delicious. And so soft, a mixture of peppermint and Mari. Better than he could have ever imagined. His hands itched to hold her, but he settled on resting one hand on her hip as the other pulled the knot from her hair.

He teased her mouth open with his tongue, needing to taste more.

And then she sighed into him. Her body melding into his.

He was a drowning man and she was his savior.

"More," she whispered against his lips, and then she took his hand from her hip and put it on her breast. Who was he to deny her? His thumb raked across her taut nipple.

She gasped, the sexiest sound ever. He backed her against the wall as his mouth explored her, and his hands took full advantage of the permission she'd just granted him.

"I don't do commitments. I have to be honest about that," he whispered in her ear as her hands squeezed his shoulders.

She tilted her head away from him and stared, her cheeks flushed. "I'm in no position to ask for something like that. I just want this, right now."

As long as they were clear on that one thing, he didn't see any reason why they shouldn't do exactly what they wanted to.

Using his other hand, he lifted her leg around his hip and pressed his hardness into her. He thought that might scare her away, for her to feel how much he needed her. She moaned and rocked against him. He stilled.

This was wrong.

This was Mari.

Hadn't he told himself only moments ago that he didn't want to risk their friendship? He should stop this before things got out of hand.

"We can't," he said. His voice was hard, but he didn't let her go. She rubbed against him.

"Why?" she asked.

"Friends. We're friends," he answered. His hand caressed her hair and his gaze snagged hers, forcing her to focus on him.

"Yes. But why can't we have the benefits? I really need the benefits."

He smiled, because damn if he didn't want the benefits as well. But they were caught up in something here. Something powerful. "No." He had to be strong enough for both of them.

She blinked and then frowned. "Oh, you don't want me?" She started to pull away, but he held her there.

How could she think that given the position they were in just then?

"I can't remember ever wanting a woman more, but this changes things. We talked about it."

"Right," she said, but she still didn't move. "But it's been six months since I had sex. You're ready. I'm ready. We do it. It's simple. We just have to keep it simple."

He leaned his forehead against hers. "What we want to do is far from simple. I'm not the guy for you. You need the forever kind. I'm a here-for-now-only type. I could get deployed tomorrow."

"Stop trying to plan a future for me. I want to be with you. Have you inside me. I don't care about tomorrow. I need this." She put her hand on him and rubbed, the friction nearly driving him mad. "Please." Then she kissed him, darting her tongue in and out of his mouth, matching time with her hand on his shaft.

When he pressed himself into her hand, she groaned, and he was lost.

A good five minutes later, he forced himself to back away. His cock was still rock-hard, but he made himself stop.

"I should go," he said. "We...you. You might

think differently tomorrow." And he couldn't get it out of his head that this one night might ruin the first good thing he'd had in years.

Her eyes were still closed, but she nodded. What a sight, with her swollen lips from his kisses, her nipples tight against her tank.

Walk away now.

"Or you could stay," she said, opening her eyes. The desire he saw there was raw and drew him back to her. "Please. I meant what I said. I can separate this," she whispered, pointing to her heart, "from what I need right now. I know the difference. Although, I should warn you. I might not be very good at it, but I want to try with you. Call it an experiment. A test mission."

"What do you mean you're not very good at it?" The last few minutes told him quite the contrary. She was a good match for him, going after what she wanted. He loved it when a woman did that.

"I, uh. I've been told I'm boring. In. Bed."

"What? Oh, the ex, right? That guy is a first-class dolt for letting you go. I wouldn't believe anything he says."

"That's so sweet, Brody. This is a one-time thing I promise you. I want to experiment…or go on a mission with someone—I want it to be you. I feel like you won't judge me."

That look, when she glanced up at him through those lashes of hers, kept him from leaving.

Walk away.

No. He had to show her that her ex didn't know what he was talking about. If he gave her nothing else, it would be the confidence that she was the sexiest woman on the planet. And she felt safe with him, she'd told him so. "We're clear? This is a bad idea."

"Already established." She reached her hand out to him.

He took it and the other and then raised them above her head. He kissed her again, his control straining. It had been so long.

"Tell me now if you want to stop."

Eyes wide, pressing her pelvis into his, she said, "No stopping. No talking. Just this." Her pert breasts teased his chest. He lifted her leg, stroking her thigh and wrapped it around his waist. She ground into him.

He was quickly losing what little control he had left.

"Need more," she demanded before kissing him long and hard. He slid his hand between them and lower into her shorts. She was wet for him and undulated against him. He had to breathe, had to slow down. But she was so tempting, so encouraging. He stroked her hard nub and she moaned. She was so tight, so hot.

"Yes," she hissed, and then she caught his tongue and sucked. He was on fire for her, her mouth might as well have been on his cock.

Could he come from just kissing her?

Her muscles tightened around his fingers and she matched his rhythm with her hips.

Yes, yes, he could. But he wouldn't. He wanted to be inside her when that happened.

"Oh," she cried out and threw back her head. He loved that she was so responsive to him. Loved the sounds she made. "Yes," her voice rasped. Her body trembled against him. He had to be inside her now, but he'd take his time, be everything to her. She was a woman to be indulged and savored.

"Brody," she gasped when he threw her over his shoulder. "What are you doing?" He took the stairs two at a time and she giggled as they bounded up the steps, his hand firm on her ass. He made it to her bedroom, where he carefully laid her on the sheets.

"Okay, Mari. I'm with you. We scratch the itch and then we're done. Back to being friends."

She nodded. Her smile alone nearly did him in. He tugged off her shorts and the silky pink thong she wore. Mari was pure heat and he had to taste her.

Before she said a word, his mouth was on her, his tongue teasing her core. Another intimate gasp from her and her fingers were running wild through his hair as he sucked and kissed. She bucked against him and he couldn't help but smile. Quiet little Mari was calling out his name and writhing. He glanced up to find her eyes hooded, and that one of her hands was squeezing her breast through her shirt.

It was the sexiest thing he'd ever seen.

Any man who didn't enjoy making love to this woman was a fool. Plain and simple.

"Brody," she panted as he teased the tiny nub relentlessly. "I've never felt like this…this…" Her thighs trembled and she rode his touch through the quake.

When she'd finally calmed, he moved up to lay next to her and kissed her passionately. After several long moments, she abruptly pulled back. "I want to taste you," she said, unzipping his jeans.

One touch of her lips and he'd lose control for sure. "Can't," he whispered. "I have to have you now, Mari, if I don't get inside you I might combust."

She burst out a laugh and he grinned. She shifted closer to him, gesturing at her top. He stripped it off her in record time and then removed her bra. Her taut, rosy nipples stole his attention as he kissed them to even tighter points. He slowed only long enough for her to shove off his jeans and sneakers. Then went the black briefs.

When she let go of him, she fell back onto the bed, pushing herself up on her elbows as she watched him, her eyes fixated on his erect cock. Control. He was at the very end of his, but he wouldn't rush this.

"Condom?" he asked. He'd never thought to bring one. Never in his wildest imagination did he think they would get to this point. Not that he hadn't considered it, but he didn't anticipate it would actually happen.

"Drawer," she told him and pointed to the side table. He nearly tore the drawer from its hinges. He ripped open the packet with his teeth and slipped the condom on.

She continued to watch him, and as she licked her lips his cock jerked. "You're amazing," he said as she tugged him to her, slipping her legs around his waist.

"You don't have to say stuff like that," she said. Her eyes glanced away. Her hair had fallen around her shoulders and her body was flush from his attention.

"Mari, hand on heart, you're one of the most stunning women I've ever met. For weeks I've thought of little more than this," he said as he teased her with the tip of him. "So many cold showers, Mari. I've dreamed of you just like this. Waiting to take me. Coming around my cock."

Her heated gaze met his. He was careful as he slid into her slowly, he wanted her to adjust to his size.

"More," she whispered fiercely. "Now."

He kissed her forehead, the tip of her nose, her sweet, full lips before he moved in and out of her, taking his time. But when she tweaked and caressed her nipples once, twice, he couldn't hold back any longer. He increased the pace, moving faster and faster.

Soon she held his face in her hands and he could see she was as lost in him as he was in her. "You feel so good," he told her as she shuddered around him. He thrust into her one last time and her back bowed, her mouth open.

"Mari," he moaned, as his release came quickly. Never had it felt so strong, so all-consuming. This wasn't just satisfaction, it was perfection. He rested on top of her, trailing kisses along her jaw, her neck, her shoulder. His cock was still throbbing inside her.

"I, um…" She bit her lip. Her big eyes focused squarely on him.

He nuzzled her gently. "What?"

"I've, um, never had an orgasm during sex before," she said as she pursed her lips. "I didn't know it could be like that."

"You've been hanging out with the wrong people." He smiled.

She reached out and touched his cheek. The movement was so intimate, his cock hardened instantly. It wasn't possible. He usually needed a lot longer than this to recover. But then he'd never been with Mari before now.

"Obviously," she said giggling. "I really didn't know…wow. And you only want to do it once? That's really disappointing because I quite liked it. I'd be game to do it again if you think you can handle it…" There was a challenge in her eyes.

"You're going to kill me, you know that?" he said. But she was right. This didn't quench his thirst. Like her, he wanted more.

She smiled sweetly.

His cock twitched again, harder than before.

Her eyes widened. "Is that…already?"

"Oh, babe, you have no idea. The first time was a bit rushed, believe me. You do that to me. Let me show you what happens when we take it slow. I mean, if we're only going to do this tonight, you really should experience it all."

Her gaze flashed with surprise.

"Slow sounds really, really good," she whispered.

He kissed her lip where she'd bitten it. "It is."

And he showed her all night long.

8

BREATHE. MARI HAD to remind herself. The small quakes in her body continued as she worried about what to do next. Had he been as affected as she was by what had just happened? After the third time in three hours, she was nestled against his chest. He pulled the comforter up over them. She was sated, exhausted yet feeling more alive than she had in years.

And thoroughly confused.

Sex had never been that…intense. That was the only way to describe it.

Is it always like that for him? How could she ask him without sounding so naive?

Sex with Gary had become more of a chore and it was always about him. When they were dating she never thought about how selfish he was. How could she? She'd been a virgin when she'd met him. In college, it wasn't as if she hadn't tried to lose her virginity, but after the third drunken frat boy passed out on her before the deed was done, she decided to focus on school instead.

She'd done her best to try and please Gary. But it hadn't been enough according to him. And now that she knew the difference between good sex—no, fantastic sex—and what wasn't, being with Gary wasn't enough for her.

Never had she imagined that would be the case for her. Brody had inspired her sexually. All she could think about was that next wave of pleasure and how she could give it right back to him. It was almost too much to comprehend.

She wasn't a cold lover at all.

It was a revelation.

Brody pushed a curl from her forehead and followed with a kiss. "You're exquisite," he murmured, before lifting her chin so that he could kiss her mouth.

Her body already ached, but it was the good kind of ache. This was a night she would never forget. He'd awakened her to things that she never knew existed.

What was she supposed to say? Thanking him profusely was wrong, though she was more grateful than she'd ever been. "I think you made me not so frigid," she told him. The words tumbled from her lips before she could stop them.

What is wrong with me? Shut up.

He smiled. "Mari, *frigid* is the last word I would ever use to describe you. It's never been so—"

"Intense?" she asked.

"Exactly. Not for me, I mean. I had no idea that it could be like that." So whatever it was that had happened between them, it was special for him, too. If it had never been like that for him either, that meant it wasn't one-sided. He was into it as much as she was.

At least there was that. Though it was truly disappointing that they only had this one night. But she'd made a promise and she wouldn't go back on that.

His hand slid down to her hip. "Are you okay?" he asked. "As you said, that was intense. That's what happens when I'm with you. I lose control."

The power his words gave her made her feel bolder. "You do that to *me*. I lost control. I, uh…"

"What?" he asked, worry furrowing his brow.

"I want to lose control again… I know," she said, pointing between them, "this is temporary. But you taught me stuff about myself tonight, I hadn't expected it. I'm inexperienced, I get that. Clearly, I missed some classes in my sexual education. So, this showed me…why can't I quit babbling?"

"Hey, you never have to worry with me." He kissed her soundly. "I like that you say what you think. You can do that all the time around me."

She nodded, grinning. "My ex was nothing like you, that's for sure."

"If he couldn't bring out your wild side in you, then he didn't deserve you. You're a knockout, Mari, and I can't get enough of you."

She didn't know if he was saying those words to be nice or what, but she appreciated so much that he wanted to make her feel good about herself. Even before this evening, he'd always been complimentary about her, how she looked, how bright she was and how hard she worked.

Bottom line: he was kind and what she needed right now.

"I don't know about you, but I could use a good soak," he said. "How about we christen that new bathtub we installed?"

She was now glad she'd forgone the traditional claw-foot tub for the behemoth one with jets. She'd warred with her design side over those jets and the need to keep things traditional in the old Victorian. In the end, the jets won. Her muscles had been really sore that day.

It hadn't occurred to her that she'd one day be sharing the tub with Brody.

Bonus.

He jumped up and swooped her into his arms. "Done." He smiled and captured her lips.

He sat her on the white marble counter while he turned on the taps. Once the tub was full, he swooped her up a second time and deposited her in the warm water. Then he slid in behind her.

"I'm going to be delightfully numb in about six

minutes," she said as he shifted her back against his chest. He used the remote on the side of the tub to switch on the jets.

They sat there in silence for a few minutes. "This is the most relaxed I've been in ages," she said.

He laughed. "You and me both. I, uh, was wondering something," he said as his erection poked at her backside. The guy was insatiable. The idea that she had that kind of effect on a man as incredible as Brody blew her mind.

"What's that?" she said, playfully ignoring his hard-on for her. It wasn't easy to do it since her body was already so tuned to his. Anticipation began to buzz through her.

His hands softly massaged her nipples. It wasn't long before they were tight peaks.

"Maybe we should ride this out, this thing between us. I'm not sure tonight will be enough to get you out of my system."

This time she was the one who laughed.

With the back of his hand he caressed her jaw and used his other hand to stroke her breast. "I know that sounds *oh so* romantic. What I meant to say was I wasn't expecting…oh, man, I'm making a mess out of this."

"Yes," she said, understanding what he wanted. "We'll play it by ear. Take each hour and day as it comes. That's kind of how I live my life now." She turned then and sat back on her heels, her knees on the bottom of the tub. "When we have our fill of one another, we'll be honest. Mature. This is a short-term fling while we fix up the house, right? We pleasure each other, seduce each other..." *Did I really just say that?* "And then we go back to being just friends."

He traced along her collarbone with his fingers and up to her jaw again. "You'll be okay with that? Just friends? I don't want to hurt you, Mari. But this can't—"

She smiled to reassure him. He was always trying to protect her. Maybe her heart would get involved, maybe it wouldn't. But she was going to treasure this time with him regardless. "Brody, I want you, I want to be with you and when it's done, it's done. I'm good. So good in fact, we should try something I've been thinking about ever since you mentioned the shower." She winked. "Will you let me do whatever I want to you?"

His eyebrow shot upward, but he nodded.

"Sit up on the ledge," she asked him.

He used his massive forearms to push himself up onto the ledge of the tub. Originally, she'd put the marble seating area there as an added convenience, but it was going to work quite well for what she had in mind.

"Lean back," she told him. When he did, his shaft popped up between them.

Her insides pulled tight at the thought of taking Brody into her mouth. He'd given her an unforgettable experience earlier; she was determined to do the same for him. "I need you to tell me the best way to do this," she said, right before she squeezed the bottom of his cock and then suckled the tip.

He moaned and placed a hand on her cheek. "Mari, what you're doing, your mouth feels so amazing. I don't need to tell you anything. You know how to—"

His words gave her confidence. She kissed him and licked his shaft, and then suckled him some more. Glancing up, she caught him watching her. With his head tilted back, he murmured her name as if he was in ecstasy. She smiled; she was doing that to him.

He called out, tangled his hands in her hair. She stopped and grinned.

This was how it was supposed to be. This give-and-take. Fifty-fifty.

"Mari, so good." One of his hands slipped from her hair to caress her shoulder. "I want you so much with that sweet little mouth of yours doing such wicked things to me."

Wicked? "What can I say, I'm a fast learner."

He groaned louder.

Yes. This was how it was supposed to be.

FOR AN HOUR Brody watched her sleep. Her relaxed face made her look almost angelic.

Yeah, an angel with a mouth made for sin. How could any man walk away from a woman like Mari? The scene in the bathtub was now number one on his top ten list of all-time favorite moments. Just thinking about her mouth on him made his cock hard again, which was why he was extricating himself from her bed. Four times in one night was enough.

Still, he hadn't had his fill.

He thought she'd be trouble and he was right. There was a connection he had with her that he hadn't had with anyone else. Maybe it was the fact that they'd begun as friends. Whatever it was due to, his feelings for her meant he'd have to rethink their arrangement.

But that wasn't the only reason he couldn't stay. He got dressed and went to leave, but stopped and stood at the door for another few minutes with his gaze on her.

The angelic blonde had no idea how amazing she was. It wasn't only the sex, which was the best ever. He could admit that. She was also a good person. Maybe that was it. So much of his life was filled with darkness and she was light. From the way she hummed when she worked, to her showing up with cold lemonade or making his favorite foods on the hot plate.

He'd never met a more giving soul.

But she's not for you. He had to remember that. Whatever it took, he would make sure that no one else around him was ever hurt, especially Mari.

The familiar pain. Another migraine. He needed to get his meds.

With one last wistful look in her direction, he then double-timed it down the stairs. He checked the back door and windows and then locked the front dead bolt with the key she'd given him so that he could get things done when she wasn't there.

Something he couldn't fully process had happened last night, and Brody wasn't convinced it was only the nature of the relationship he had with Mari that had changed.

He'd changed.

And there wasn't anything he could do about it. Because tomorrow he'd be back to take whatever she could give him.

Hell. He had a new demon and her name was Mari.

9

MARI WAS HUMMING as she put away some files when Abbott walked in. Her friend looked like she might have partied a bit too much the night before.

"Late night?" Mari asked, slamming the file drawer shut with her hip.

Abbott flinched. "Stop that. There's no reason to be so loud. And why are you so cheerful. You either got busy with that Marine, or the Colsons finally signed their contract."

Mari grinned. "Both."

Abbott's eyes flashed wide. "Wait." She held up her hand. She left the office and came back with two cups of coffee. She placed one cup in front of Mari, who was sitting behind her desk, and then she sipped from the other.

"Abbott—"

Her friend held up a finger. "Two more minutes."

After half a cup of coffee, she smiled. "Okay, yay

on the stuffy Colsons. Though, you know they're going to be a huge pain in the butt. Can you imagine them making a decision on the redesign of their kitchen when it took them two months just to sign their contract?"

"Which is why I had a stipulation added that they have one week to make a decision on any idea presented to them. They actually agreed to it."

"That's brilliant."

"I thought so."

"All right." Abbott took another sip of coffee. "So you slept with the Marine. I'm going to throw you a party since you finally let go and had some fun."

Mari laughed. "I admit I haven't been this relaxed in years. However, I refuse to be one of those women who kisses and tells."

"Oh, no. You are so gonna spill," Abbott insisted.

She shook her head. "Talking about it, I don't know, it takes some of the fantasy away."

Abbott sighed. "I get that, but you have to give me something. Was he amazing?"

"I'll say only this—I had no idea how much I didn't know. He's taught me a lot. And, I knew before, but now it's been confirmed, breaking up with Gary was the best thing that ever happened to me. The. Best. Thing. Now that I know what can be, I'll never settle for less."

Abbott whistled. "Look at you! I'm happy for you. It's about time."

"True that."

They both laughed.

"Is it serious?" Abbott leaned forward still cupping the coffee close to her face.

Mari cocked her head. "No. We've both been really clear about that. I'm not ready for anything serious. He's not into commitments, so it's kind of perfect for both of us. We're having fun. That's it."

Abbott's hand went to her chest. "My little Mari is all grown up and having excellent casual sex with a hot Marine. I couldn't be any prouder."

Mari rolled her eyes. "So I had this crazy idea, and I might need your help."

"Crazier than having steamy sex with your boy toy?"

"Stop. Yes. I'm going to throw a Valentine's party for family, friends and a few of our clients. Maybe even a few of our potential clients."

Abbott frowned. "I hate Valentine's Day."

"Me, too, which is why I thought we could make this more a friendly gathering."

"Where is this shindig supposed to take place?"

"My house."

Her friend nearly dropped the coffee cup.

"But Valentine's Day is a few weeks away."

She wagged her finger. "You haven't been by in a while. With Brody's help, it's all come together so fast. The man can do anything."

"Wow. You're into him. I can tell. I don't care how casual you think things are, you're so into him."

Maybe she was. But when Brody grew tired of what they had, she would let go. Fast. She'd promised him she would. She'd promised herself.

It would hurt, but at the first sign she saw of him losing interest, she would walk away. She had to, for her own good and for his.

MARI AND BRODY stood outside the high-rise building where her ex's engagement party was being thrown. The wind had picked up and a thunderstorm threatened. Her red dress whipped around her thighs and she had to hold it down with her hands. It wasn't that she was worried about seeing Gary and his new fiancée again. It was that some of their old friends would be there. People who had treated her like a social pariah when he'd dumped her, as if she'd done something wrong.

The lobby doorman pushed open the glass door. Brody put his hand lightly on her hip to guide her into the fancy building. Funny how in the last week since they'd first made love, she'd grown to crave his touch. Her body leaned into his, without her even thinking about it. There was strength in him and never had she needed it more.

"We don't have to go in," Mari said as they rode up in the elevator.

"No. We don't. You have nothing to prove." Brody took her hand in his. "You look great in that dress and those heels. All I can think about is stripping them off of you. Frankly, I'm okay with leaving, if that's what you want. What I want is to be inside you."

It was as if a passel of butterflies was let loose low in her belly. "Brody," she scolded, and slapped at him playfully. "Now I won't be able to think about anything else. I can hardly breathe."

He chuckled and then caressed her jawline with the back of his hand. He did that often. She loved how he was always touching her. Having his hands on her, even now, made her think of him filling her so completely.

"You're all I think about," he whispered. "And now I'm hard as a rock. You can't talk like that and expect me to stand idly by. I could press you up against the wall right here and—" The doors to the elevator dinged open. He took her hand and led her from the elevator. In the hallway, people milled around and the apartment door at the end of the corridor was open.

"Twenty minutes," he said as they made their way to Gary's. "Then I'm taking you home. That's about as long as I can wait to have you."

Heat pooled at her core. It was all she could do not to haul him back to the elevator so they could go home and make love.

As they neared the open door, his arm went around her shoulders. "We're going to show your ex that you've moved on and that he's pretty much the dumbest guy who's ever lived."

On the inside, she was doing a happy dance.

Every once in a while Brody would say something like that and make her wonder what life might be like with a man like him—permanently. One who treated her with kindness and satisfied every desire she had. Not that they were really together. This was a friends-with-benefits situation, which she kept having to remind herself of, but still...

"You've got this," Brody said as he guided her through the entryway.

They were met by Annalise, the new fiancée, who wore a tight, neon green dress with cutouts and very high heels.

How does she breathe in that outfit? There wasn't an ounce of fat anywhere in those cutouts.

Mari sighed. No matter. Even if her time with Brody wasn't long-term, she had moved forward with her life. She didn't need a man—any man— to define her. But if she was going to have fun and awesome sex, she might as well do it with the handsome, well-built Marine.

She took a deep breath and smiled.

Annalise's eyes went straight to Brody. "Hi," she said breathily without even glancing at Mari. "I'm so very glad you could make it. I remember meeting you—I mean, who would forget you, but I'm afraid I have forgotten your name."

His eyebrow lifted. "Brody," he said. "And this is my girlfriend, Mari. Remember, she used to date your fiancé?"

Annalise frowned as she spared Mari a quick

glance. "Yes. I remember now." She waved at them and then gestured at the room. "How grown up are all of us that we can hang out like this?"

Mari wasn't feeling grown up at all. Annalise's hand had landed on Brody's biceps. She was about ready to tell the woman to get her hand off of his arm. Hadn't she taken enough from Mari? Well, she'd done her a favor. After being with Brody for a short time, she couldn't believe she'd almost ended up with a creep like Gary. Still, the woman needed to stop touching Brody.

She cleared her throat and looped her arm through his, effectively removing him from the other woman's clutches.

Annalise's lips formed a pout as if Mari had taken away her favorite toy.

"Yeah, so…my Gary is over at the bar," Annalise said. "You guys should go say hello. He was just telling me the other day that he doubted you would show up. He'll be so surprised."

I bet. Mari'd prefer to avoid ol' Gary, but she and Brody could at least get a drink and maybe check out the view.

Brody kissed Mari's cheek. "Babe, we need to hurry and do whatever it is we're going to do here. We're down to eighteen minutes."

She smiled and her breath caught yet again. The man did dangerous things to her body with mere words. "We could go now."

He leaned down and nipped her ear. "Or, we could do it now. Again and again," he murmured.

She couldn't seem to catch her breath, it took her a long moment before she replied. "Hmm, who's the one being bad now? But really, I'm ready to leave, we can—"

"Mari?" She instantly recognized the voice. She turned to find Gary's mother standing before her. "Darling girl, how are you?" she gushed and kissed the air near Mari's face. The thing was, Mari had always liked her ex's mom. Unlike Gary, his mother was pretty down to earth. She came from old money, but she didn't put on any airs and graces. A Southern belle from Georgia, she had a way of telling it like it was, but it still sounded sweet.

"I'm great," Mari answered truthfully. For the first time in her life, she meant those words. Her life had been a nightmare for the last few months, but being with Brody had been good for her. She'd learned so much about herself and her body, and when they did part, she would be better off for having been with him. Even though it might break her heart.

"I could disown him for what he did to you," his mother said, "and then he attaches himself to her. There's not a part of that woman that hasn't been surgically enhanced for no good reason. She was actually bragging about her butt implants earlier. Can you imagine? Harold and I don't understand. You're such a lovely young woman. Honest and genuine."

"That's nice of you to say." Mari smiled. "And I do miss you and Harold. But your son actually did me a huge favor. If I was still with Gary, I would have never met Brody." She nodded toward the man holding her close. Those words were true, as well. The heat from Brody's body poured strength into her. With him at her side, she felt invincible. "Brody, if you haven't guessed yet, this is Gary's mother, Helen."

Brody reached out his right hand and said, "It's great to meet you, ma'am."

Helen's eyes widened and she smiled. "Oh, my, you are a handsome one, and I'd hazard military with those muscles and that haircut."

"Marine, ma'am, Lieutenant Brody Williams, and thank you for the kind words."

"It's deserved. My, my. Mari, you've done well for yourself. And that voice, so low and husky. You are a dreamboat, Lieutenant."

Mari chuckled and so did Brody. "As I told you…" The older woman's eyebrow shot up. "His father and I aren't exactly ecstatic about his choices of late. He was silly to let you get away."

"I couldn't agree more," Brody put in. "But I have to admit I'm grateful. My time with Mari has been some of the best in my life. She's helped me figure out a lot of things and made my world a better place to be." When he glanced down at her, her heart caught in her throat. He'd meant those words. She could tell from the sincerity in his eyes.

"You're bright as well as handsome. Smart enough to grab our Mari up. She's a superb young woman, and she's going places. I've always said that."

"Don't I know it," Brody said as he kissed her hair. "She's special."

She glanced up at him and he gave her a look that made her believe the words yet again. Her desire for him skyrocketed.

No. *He's playing a role.* And he's really, really good at it. That was it. All the goodness and better-world stuff was an act.

Do not fall for this. He's your friend who you have awesome sex with, and that's it.

Then he kissed her lightly on the lips. Every nerve ending in her body tingled. Too late, she was under the spell that was Brody Williams. The man's lips were dangerous. His hand slipped down to her hip, and it was all she could do not to crawl onto him right there in the middle of the party and wrap her legs around him. She'd done it so many times in the last week. They'd worked hard on the house, but they'd played hard every night, and still she wanted more. He'd touch her, or smile, and just like that, her body ached with the need for him.

Like it did right now in the middle of this party.

Yep, she had it bad.

"Yes, Mari, you've done quite well for yourself." She barely heard the woman. Her attention was focused on Brody. When he favored her with one of his crooked smiles, her knees almost gave out.

"You kids have fun," Helen said as she sauntered away, giving them a knowing smile.

"I can't wait eleven more minutes," Brody said into her ear. "I need to have you now."

"Well, look who is here." Michael, one of Gary's business partners, walked up to them. He'd always been nice to her, and was one of the people who called to check on her after the breakup.

"Hey, Michael," she said, stepping out of Brody's arms to hug the other man.

Michael hugged her back and then held her out at arm's length.

"You look to die for. I could eat you up, Mari. You are delicious."

She thought she heard a growl. Brody was playing the possessive male to the hilt, and she was falling hard for it.

It was a huge turn-on to be wanted. And she had no doubt Brody wanted her—at least sexually. And for now, she was fine with that.

"This is Lieutenant Brody Williams," she said, introducing him to Michael. They shook hands. He slipped his arm around her.

"So, Mari, I have some folks who are looking for an interior designer. I wanted to send them over to you, but I wasn't sure after, uh, everything that happened you'd want to still do business with us."

Mari shrugged. "I don't see why not?" Michael was an architect at Gary's firm and handled most of the high-end clients.

"Excellent. Maybe we could meet for lunch one day next week."

Brody's hand was on her back, propelling her away. "Text me on Monday," she called out to him as she and Brody moved away.

"That was business," she grumbled, but she didn't mean it. Her Marine had an intense gaze.

"He touched you," he growled again. "And he asked you out to lunch with me standing right there. I don't like it."

She laughed. "You're playing the possessive boyfriend really well."

"Mari, I'm not joking. I don't care how it makes me seem, I don't want you spending time alone with that guy. He wants you in the worst way."

"Brody, don't be silly. I've been friends with him for a long time."

"Yep, and you're friends with me and in two minutes I will be inside you."

This time, she faltered. Her knees wobbled. "We can just leave," she whispered.

"No." He guided her through the throng of partygoers. "I can't wait that long."

"Hey, Mari." One of her old friends came up to talk to her, but all she could do was wave.

"No stopping," Brody said in her ear. "You have one minute before I bend you over the table in the middle of this room and rip those panties off in front of everyone."

Heat infused her body from head to toe. She was so aroused, ready. "Can we? Here?"

"We can," he said. The huskiness in his voice gave her power. He needed her. When he glanced down at her with that look in his eyes, the one he got right before he was about to possess her body and soul, she all but climaxed then and there.

Someone else called out to her, but she didn't turn around. A new sense of urgency filled her. She needed him, too. Once they were alone in the hallway, he started opening doors. The second one on the right they discovered was a guest bedroom. "This will do," he said, and she followed. He shut the door behind them and didn't bother switching on a light. It was pitch-black, but their mouths and hands found one another. He hiked up her dress and pushed aside her panties.

She gasped. His long fingers slid into her slick heat, and his tongue plundered her mouth. She unzipped him and stroked his shaft. "I want this just as much as you do," she said, panting. When she squeezed him, he hissed.

"Turn around and put your hands on the door."

She did as he'd asked. Next there was the sound of the condom packet ripping. He paused, but only for a second. Then he entered her from behind.

She quickly matched his pulse-pounding rhythm. She loved every pressing thrust as he pistoned harder and harder. The growing feeling deep inside her overtook her like a gathering storm that she couldn't outrun. Here—with Brody—she didn't want to. Instead, she wanted everything he could give her.

"Touch yourself," he said, as his fingers teased her nipples through her dress.

They'd done so many things together, but not that. He took one hand off her breast to put her hand on her slick heat. Then he nipped her ear, pressed kisses to her neck.

She wanted to giggle, to let loose all the emotion and happiness bubbling up within her.

Never in her life had she felt so elated. Touching herself like this was something she'd only done alone, most recently to thoughts of what Brody was doing to her now.

He pulled out, his tip poised at her opening. "You can do it," he mouthed next to her ear.

She worked her fingers slowly at first, but then quicker over her nub. The sensation of him thrusting behind her and the friction of her touch brought her to orgasm in seconds.

As he captured her cry with his mouth, he caressed her breasts, her hips, her thighs, sending waves of pleasure from her core through every inch of her. Still he claimed her, until her body quickened again. This time they sped over the edge together, her bones melding into his as if they were one. The only thing that kept her upright was him supporting her.

"Mine," he said as he found his release. "You're

mine, Mari." She'd never felt so strong, knowing that meant he was hers in kind. It was heady and wonderful. His body shuddered around her.

"And this is the guest room," a voice said from the other side of the door. Oh, no. Someone was about to find them.

She should have been mortified about the possibility, but she didn't care. She was so happy, so fulfilled. She so, so didn't care.

Brody nuzzled her hair, gently let go of her and then righted himself. She slipped her panties into place and smoothed down her dress. The absurdity of the situation hit her as funny and she slapped a hand over her mouth to stop from laughing out loud. The voices faded away and the door remained shut.

She faced Brody and he wrapped his arms around her, kissing her again and again. "That was…" He hesitated, seemingly at a loss for words.

"Amazing," she filled in. "I've never had sex where someone might walk in. That was daring." So not vanilla.

"I feel like I should say I'm sorry, but I'm not." He smiled and his fingers trailed across her face tenderly. He could have all the time he wanted for this; this she loved.

"No, don't apologize. That was fun, Brody. Unexpected, but fun. And we've stayed more than the required twenty minutes. Take me home, please, Marine. We haven't christened the dining room yet, or the pantry or—"

"Whatever you want, babe." He kissed her on the lips. She wanted more. When he lifted his head, he said, "But just so you know, for the rest of the night I'm taking my time with you."

She shivered with anticipation.

Before he opened the door, he swept her into another long kiss. They finally came up for air. "While we're doing this, Mari, promise me that you're mine and only mine. I can't handle another man touching you."

"I promise you it's not like that with Michael. He's like a brother to me. But I'm flattered, Brody. I still can't believe this is happening between us. Whatever it is. Exclusive is good and it works both ways, right?"

He held her close. "Yes, it does. Until we are done."

She didn't want to think about the done part. Instead, she concentrated on how his touch was sending shivers down her spine.

It was crazy. She'd never been this responsive to any man. Of course, they'd established she hadn't been hanging out with the right men. But she had a feeling Brody was one of a kind. That hurt. One day soon, when the house was finished, it would be over between them. Or he might get transferred or even deployed overseas. She forced those sad thoughts from her mind.

Don't get caught up in the future. Enjoy today. Yes. That's what she had to remember.

After they made sure their clothes were in order,

he swung open the bedroom door and they ran smack into Gary.

Mari started giggling. She couldn't help it. Even though they'd sorted themselves out, there was no doubt from her disheveled hair and the heat warming her cheeks that they'd been up to some very naughty things.

Very, very naughty.

"Hey, man," Brody said to her ex. "Again, thank you. She's the best thing that's ever happened to me. Oh, and you've got some great walls in this place. Ultra soundproof."

Gary stared at them, his jaw hanging open. He glanced from her to Brody and then back again. He knew exactly what they'd been doing.

"We've got to go," Brody said. "Can't keep my hands off her, practically made love to her right in front of all your guests." Then he pulled her through the party as if they were rushing away from a fire.

Maybe they were, because Mari was burning hotter than she ever had before.

Danger. Danger.

She just didn't care. Whatever time she had with Brody, she would make the most of it.

10

SOMETHING WAS WRONG and Brody had no idea what it was. As they reached the pier where the CO's rented yacht was docked, Mari was continuing to be quiet.

After the party at her ex's on Friday, he and Mari had made love for most of the night. She'd been fine before she'd drifted off to sleep. But that was hours ago. Now it was Saturday afternoon, and ever since he'd picked her up at her house, she'd been silent. For the life of him he couldn't figure out what he'd done, but he was sure it was bad.

"Are you okay? You don't seem like yourself," he asked for what felt like the hundredth time.

"I'm fine." The slight shake in her hand said something different.

"The CO likes you, and you met almost everyone who's here at the picnic," he said, trying to encourage her. "If we weren't dating he'd probably be all over you. Every time I run in to him at the base, he asks how you are." He frowned. He didn't like the idea of anyone being hot for Mari except him. Yesterday when the CO had cornered him to make sure Brody was bringing Mari on the boat, he'd almost told him to get lost. But he also didn't like the idea of having to dig latrines for the next millennia, so he'd kept his thoughts to himself.

He wasn't sure what had happened to him exactly, but he felt protective toward her, possessive even. He didn't get that way over every woman. The line between them pretending and the real thing was long gone, he suddenly realized. He cared about her. Didn't want her dating anyone else.

That's not good.

"It's not that. We should just go," she said, reaching for the car door handle. He had the urge to stop her. Instead, he jumped out quickly to help her down from the truck. Then he leaned in behind the seat to get the present she'd chosen and wrapped the day before. She wouldn't say what it was, only that it was something the CO would like.

He followed her down the ramp to where the yacht was moored. The late afternoon sun was warm, and a gentle breeze lifted the skirt of the blue dress she wore. She nervously pushed it down.

"You are so pretty," he said.

She gave him a quick smile, but it wasn't her normal sunny one.

"If you aren't feeling well, I can make excuses. I'll drop off the present and we can go."

"No," she said abruptly. Then she put on the fake smile. "I mean, we're here. We might as well say hello." That smile would have worked on anyone else, but he'd spent enough time with her to know it wasn't genuine. When she got to the yacht, he assisted her across the ramp. Again, her hand shook.

Why won't she tell me what's wrong?

Carissa waved them on board. She was in white shorts that should have been illegal and a rhinestone-covered bikini top. He preferred Mari's dress. The blue brought out the color in her eyes and it molded perfectly to her figure.

"Everyone is in there," Carissa said as she pointed toward a large living space. Then she looked past him and waved furiously. He glanced back to see his buddy Ben Peterson. Poor guy, he was in for it now. The CO's daughter had moved on.

It was crowded in the main area and there wasn't much seating. Mari seemed even more tense than she had been before they'd gotten on board the boat. They said hello to the CO and then took a tour of the massive yacht. It was stunning.

There were about fifty people there, the senior officers from the base and their significant others, along with some of the CO's friends. After the tour Brody got caught up in a conversation with Mark and Gray about the new fuel pumps going into the Vipers.

Mari excused herself to go to the ladies' room. He felt bad about her being excluded from the conversation, and made a note to himself to be sure they talked about things that might interest her when she returned. When she hadn't come back in twenty minutes, he went to look for her. She wasn't in any of the bathrooms or in the main area. He checked the bedrooms and then climbed the stairs up to the deck, slightly panicked. Maybe she'd gotten off before they left port. He hoped not.

He and Mari never should have boarded the boat. He'd known something wasn't right.

He'd almost given up when he found her sitting on one of the lounge chairs off the central deck with her knees tucked under her chin. She didn't look good. Her glowing skin was slightly green and there was a white rim around her luscious pink lips.

Seasick. He'd seen it before. Even the toughest Marine could get hit with it. They were just out of the harbor and the yacht sluiced through the water, barely rocking, but she was feeling it.

He sat down on the chair next to hers. "Why didn't you tell me?"

"What?" She kept her eyes on the water beyond the railing.

"That you either hate the water or boats."

She shrugged.

"Or both," he mused. Her dress was over her legs and she had her arms crossed over her knees with her chin on them.

She sighed. "I didn't want to disappoint you. And it's a big boat, I thought I could handle it. I wanted you to impress your CO." She lowered her voice on the last part.

"You could never disappoint me, Mari. We could have stayed home in bed and it would have been a lot more fun."

She tensed.

Was she regretting that they'd taken things further than they'd planned? Their relationship had hit a new level that caught him off guard sometimes. Such as, he always wanted to be with her. That had never happened before.

But they'd both been lonely and he truly believed that it was a good compromise for them to find some affection with one another. Their time was limited, and it was supposed to be casual. Maybe she thought it should be more.

He'd just admitted to himself that he was feeling a bit possessive of her. Or maybe she was done. He didn't blame her. She didn't normally have sex at parties. And the people there were her friends, or at least had been. She'd wanted to impress them, not run out with mussed hair and her face wearing the heat from their lovemaking. He should apologize again.

"Last night, I shouldn't have been so, ah, that is…"

"It's not that. It's nothing," she said.

He grasped her chin lightly and held her face

close to his. "Talk to me, please. You've been upset since this morning."

"I told you it doesn't matter." She pulled away.

But it did. She was backing away from him and he didn't like it. "It matters to me. I don't want you to be upset. Obviously I've done something stupid, but I have no idea what. If it's about last night, I apologize for how I acted. I always lose control when you're—"

"Don't you dare apologize for last night, it was wonderful. I enjoyed every minute."

So it was something he'd done afterward.

"I told you I'm not good at relationships, but I thought our arrangement was working out well. I care about you, so tell me how I can fix it."

She shook her head. "You're right. I'm not feeling well. It's kind of silly."

He took her hand in his. "It isn't silly to me, but hold on two seconds. I think I have a solution for the first problem." He found one of the waitstaff and explained the situation. A few minutes later he handed Mari two pills and a bottle of water.

"Take these."

"I don't think taking anything right now is advisable."

"Trust me. These are for nausea." She swallowed the pills and had a sip of water.

Then he grabbed the plastic packet out of his pocket and pulled off one of the patches. After lifting her hair, he placed the patch behind her ear.

"This will help, as well. Maybe even faster than the pills. It's an antinausea patch."

She shivered. He took off his suit jacket and wrapped it around her shoulders. "Now talk to me," he said. He wracked his brain trying to figure out what he'd done between last night and this afternoon.

"It's not a big deal."

"Oh, but it is. Let's always be honest with one another. We have been so far. Tell me what's bothering you."

She shrugged again. "You never stay," she said, glancing away. "It's not the end of the world, but kind of makes me feel— It's dumb. I have no right to expect anything from you."

It took him a moment to figure out what she was talking about. "Mari, I leave after you fall asleep every night in order to protect you."

She glanced back at him, frowning. "What?"

"I have night terrors. It's— I've had them since— I told you that I lost a lot of my men—my friends— in a crash. It's messed with my brain. I can't sleep and I wake up all hours of the night, sometimes violently. I've punched holes in walls and bloodied my hands before I ever woke up and figured out what was happening.

"I'd never want to hurt you. So once you fall asleep, I slip out. It's all so I don't accidentally harm you in some way. Trust me, leaving you every night is the toughest thing I have to do these days. There's nothing I'd love more than to wake up with you in my arms, but it isn't safe."

She blessed him with one of her genuine Mari-lights-up-the-world grins. "I never thought of that," she said. "You don't talk about what happened, not that you need to with me. I'm still so insecure sometimes, and I'm sure I'm letting the past color whatever this craziness is that we have. I thought maybe I looked really bad in the morning or you were secretly embarrassed about being with me."

"Never." He pulled her into his lap. "I will tell you this every single day and it will be the truth. Mari, any man would be proud to have you on his arm. I don't care what anyone else thinks. Whether you're wearing fancy party clothes, or that old Cowboys jersey and those tiny shorts, you're sexy. I especially love you in those tiny shorts."

"You're so bad."

He grinned.

"I've read about PTSD, Brody, but I've never met anyone who had it. Do you go to counseling?"

"I did when I first got back." But then he'd moved to Corpus and hadn't found another support group. Maybe it was time he tried.

He felt bad that Mari didn't think he cared enough about her to stay through the night. It was that he cared too much. He had noticed since he'd been with her that he hadn't been having the nightmares or the headaches as often. He usually fell into bed exhausted by the time he made it back to his place. He'd even cut down his runs to one a day because he was making love with Mari every night. She was as insatiable as he was.

"We could try," he said.

She frowned as if she didn't understand.

"Me sleeping over. You just have to promise that if I start moving around or yelling, you can't touch me or try to wake me up. You need to get away. If I ever hurt you, I'd never forgive myself." He rubbed his fingers along her cheek.

She wrapped her arms around his neck. "I'll be careful, I promise. I hate that you have these nightmares. You've been through so much already."

"It's the job and the sense of duty I feel. Sometimes there can be side effects." People often asked him if he had regrets. Never about joining the military, but always about the friends he'd lost while serving. He was a proud Marine, and he'd do whatever it took to protect his country. But he did miss his colleagues.

"Still. I appreciate you and what you've sacrificed. And now that I know why, I'm good with whatever makes you feel comfortable. You don't have to sleep over."

"Are you afraid of me now?" He couldn't blame her.

"No. I would never be frightened of you. But I don't want to push you into anything, especially if you're worried about it.

"We'll try," he said. It did worry him that he

might unintentionally hurt her. But he wanted her to know it wasn't just sex between them. Not that what they were doing was anything serious. But he cared for her.

A lot.

In the last few weeks, Mari had become the center of his world. For all his talk about keeping things casual, he was falling for her. That hadn't ever happened before. Her happiness was important to him. More than his own.

Crud.

"Hey, you two lovebirds," Ben called out. "Carissa sent me to get you guys. The CO is cutting his birthday cake."

"We'll be right in."

"So I told you my secret." Brody kissed her cheek. "You tell me why you hate the boats and water so much."

She sighed. "It's more of a combo thing. I love swimming. The water doesn't bother me as long as I can put my feet on the ground. When I was about ten, I was kayaking down some rapids with my family. I struggled to get some air, right away the current picked me up. It was going too fast. I hit my head on a rock and nearly drowned."

"You had to have been scared to death."

She nodded. "I was. And then I blacked out. Abbott, who works with me, pulled me to safety. We've been best friends since kindergarten. When I moved here, she did as well. She was my roommate for years. If it wasn't for her, I wouldn't be alive. It's nothing like you've been through, but I've pretty much avoided boats until today."

The idea of something happening to her tugged at his gut. He hugged her and kissed her forehead. "I'm really thankful for her right now. And you should have told me. I could have come alone, or we could have stayed home and worked on the house. As much as I want to impress the CO, you're more important, especially if being here makes you uncomfortable."

She gave him a warm smile. "You are the sweetest. I'll be honest I didn't expect that the yacht would actually leave the harbor. I've been to parties before where it just stays at the dock. But I'm okay. I have you." She kissed his jaw and his cock grew hard. "I know you'll keep me safe."

"You can count on it." He had her in his arms and he hugged her tightly, losing himself in her warmth. He would keep her safe, but he wasn't so sure about his heart.

MARI HELD FAST to Brody's arm as they disembarked from the boat. The pills he'd given her, along with a bit of champagne, had helped tamp down her nerves. But never in her life had she been so glad to see dry land.

Once they were in his truck, Brody turned to her. "Are you up for another adventure?"

No. But he seemed so excited and she didn't want

to disappoint him. "What do you have in mind?" She liked that he pushed her out of her comfort zone, and honestly he hadn't steered her wrong yet.

"Tomorrow night I'd like to take you somewhere."

"Like on a date? I thought we, you know, just did this for appearances." As she said the word she wished she hadn't. It always made her think of when this might all end. And that scared the heck out of her because she liked Brody. Probably a little too much.

He turned off the truck and took her hands in his. "I like spending time with you," he said. "Whether we're fixing up the house, or like tonight, I just like having you near."

"I like hanging out with you, too. But you don't have to do extra stuff to get me to sleep with you. I'm counting that as a bonus." There, that sounded nice and casual.

He chuckled. "Mari, that's the best bonus I've had in a really long time. A *really* long time. But what I want to show you is something that's a part of me. An important part and I want to share it with you."

She clapped her hands together like a little kid getting some candy. "So what is it? Now I'm all intrigued."

He kissed her lightly on the lips. She wanted so much more. "You'll have to wait until tomorrow."

She just remembered. "I have plans tomorrow, but I'll be free in the afternoon."

He sat back and frowned.

Maybe he thought she had a date, but they'd already said they were exclusive. "With Abbott. She's my assistant at work. We have to do a walk-through on a new client's house, and then we're going shopping. I've been getting so much exercise with you at night the last couple of weeks that I need to pick up some new jeans. Before I met you I could barely fit in them, and now they're too big."

He laughed. "Side benefit of the bonus."

"Right?" She laughed with him. "I could postpone the shopping, but I really need them. And this client has rescheduled on me twice already."

"Go buy your jeans, and I'll pick you up at the house say around four tomorrow afternoon. That should give us plenty of time."

He started the truck and drove toward home. "One thing…" His tone was serious this time.

"What is it?" she asked.

"Tonight, I'm going to stay at my place. I know what we talked about, but after this thing tomorrow. I think…we can make it better. That doesn't make a lick of sense to you right now, but once you see the surprise, it might. Ben actually made the suggestion."

She leaned over the console of the truck and squeezed his shoulder. "It's okay. Really, Brody. I don't want you to feel any kind of pressure. Now that I understand why you were doing it, I'm grateful. I don't have that much experience with guys. So I wasn't sure what to think."

He took her hand and kissed her fingers.

"It's weird," he said.

"What?"

"Talking." He chuckled. "I've shared more with you in the last few weeks. Talked more than I have probably in a couple of years."

"I should confess, I feel the same way. I'm comfortable with you. I can be myself and you don't seem to mind that I'm a tad unique. In the past, I was always worried that I'd turn a guy off if I didn't like the same movies or music that he did. It's dumb. I tried to make myself into whatever he wanted me to be."

"You're kind of awesome the way you are." The breath caught in her throat. The man made her total mush inside. Absolute total mush.

"You're pretty awesome yourself."

Yep. She had it bad for Brody. A wickedly bad case of lust, or… When this was over, the pain would be a hundred times worse than it had been with Gary. But she would never regret this experience. Brody had given her so much and she didn't think he had a clue.

Yep. Heartbreak was ahead, but she was sticking with her plan to enjoy every moment she could with her Marine.

11

"So, you're doing it like bunnies and that's why you need skinny jeans?" Abbott said a little too loudly in the coffee shop where they stopped to get their iced chais with espresso. After her long night with Brody—he hadn't left until the wee hours of the morning—she needed a little pick-me-up.

"Abbott, not so loud. But yes," Mari whispered as they sat down at a table near the window. "He's so… I can't even explain it. Strong, kind and generous. Today, while I'm here, he's at my house sanding down the banisters and the stairs so we can stain them. But at the same time I'm scared."

"Your life just sucks," Abbott said sarcastically. "A hot guy who gives you multiple orgasms and fixes your house. Oh, the horrors."

"I told you, it's all temporary. Every part of it. And I'm okay with that. At least I have been, but now he's spoiled me for other men. How do you go from Brody to anyone else? I mean, I was with Gary and I thought he was okay." Though, now she understood that she'd never loved him, and he certainly hadn't cared about her. They'd been going through the motions of what couples were supposed to do. It was no wonder he went off and found someone else. Not that he still wasn't a jerk, but she understood a little better.

"You're falling for him hard," Abbott said. She picked up Mari's phone and glanced at the pic they'd taken on the yacht the night before. "I don't think I've ever seen you this happy, and you were on a *boat*. You hate boats."

Mari laughed. "I know, right? Once we talked and he took me inside, I actually had a good time. I don't want to get on another one anytime soon, but I always have fun when I'm with him."

Abbott nodded. Then she turned the phone toward Mari. "The way he's looking at you, I'd say he's fallen hard as well."

Mari shook her head. "Nah. He's just a—" She glanced down at the picture. While she was smiling from ear to ear, he was watching her with this passionate look in his eyes. Was it possible? Was he into her as much as she was into him?

In the last two weeks, they'd progressed pretty fast. It might be one of those things that burned out quickly. She didn't have enough experience with affairs or flings to know what to expect.

"Oh, girl. You are too far gone," Abbott said.

"You guys should talk. Maybe this temporary thing might not be so…temporary."

Mari bit her lip and then shrugged. "No. It's hot and heavy right now, but he's made it clear on several occasions that he's not a forever kind of guy. I get from what he's said about his dad, who has been married several times, that he feels like he's cut from the same cloth. He doesn't ever want to get married. And while that's okay for me right now, eventually I do want to settle down with someone."

There was no way she'd be able to do that with Brody. He'd admitted he cared for her, but this thing between them would wind down. At the moment, it was too much, too fast.

"I don't know. Maybe he just hasn't met the right woman. Maybe you're the one who takes Lieutenant Brody Williams off the market."

No. She wouldn't let herself think like that. And she wouldn't forget a minute of it. When it was over, and it was probably coming soon, she'd walk away with her head held high knowing she was better off for having met Brody.

You keep telling yourself that.

INSTEAD OF USING his key like he always did, Brody knocked on the door this time. He wanted Mari to feel like this was a real date. It was. Last night, when he realized how upset she was about his not staying over, he decided to show her how much he cared.

He didn't know where this thing between them was going, but he wasn't ready for it to end. The house was almost done, and they'd given themselves that time limit, but he was far from finished with her. In fact, Mari was the first woman he'd thought maybe he could forever be with. They were burning pretty hot, but the more time he had with her, the more he wanted.

He sometimes wished they could spend even more time together. He'd never been like that with a woman. He'd only been on more than one date with a handful of women, and never more than two dates. But with Mari, it was never enough. Sometimes he worried he might overwhelm her.

So tonight, he was showing her they could do what regular people did. Go out, have a good time. Well, maybe not *regular*. The surprise he had planned wasn't something most people ever had the opportunity to do. He knocked again when she didn't answer.

"Just a minute." He heard her call and then rushed down the steps. In true Mari style, she was running late. That sort of thing used to bug him, but she was worth the wait.

She proved it when she opened the door. She had a sky-blue blouse that dipped down to show the top curve of her beautiful breasts. And her dark jeans looked as though they'd been tailored for her.

"Oh." Her hand flew to her chest. "You look,

wow. Brody, you take my breath away. You're so handsome in that sweater and jeans."

"I was just about to tell you how gorgeous you look, Mari. Those jeans, all I can think about is taking them off you."

She shrugged. "We could always stay here, but then I'd miss out on your surprise."

"True." He brought his right hand from behind his back. "These are for you." He knew she liked pink and white, so he'd had the florist put together a special bouquet.

"I've never received flowers before." She took them from him and then sniffed. "And they smell so good. You didn't have to do this."

"I wanted to. Put them in water and then we need to go." He followed her into the kitchen, unable to keep his eyes off her ass. "Those jeans," he muttered.

Mari turned and smiled at him. "So you like?" Then she wiggled her butt in a cute little dance.

And there he went, hard as steel. It didn't take much with her. He grabbed her elbow gently and pulled her back against him, then rubbed himself against her tight little butt. "This is what you do to me, Mari, every time I see you."

A moan escaped as she leaned into him. Her body was made for him. He'd figured that out the first night they'd made love.

"Go," he said, gently pushing her away. "You moan like that again and we'll never make it out of here." She gave him a playful wink, but then moved on to the kitchen to get a vase.

Twenty minutes later they were at the base. When he checked in at the front gate, she eyed him curiously. "Are you going to show me where you work?"

He nodded. "That's part of the surprise." He put the visitor badge on her chest, spending a bit more time there than he should. Then he kissed her.

For some reason, he was nervous. Maybe it was sharing this part of himself, or maybe it was what he felt he needed to tell her. He drove them to the hangar.

She took a deep breath and put a hand on his arm. "This is so exciting. A real look into the life of Lieutenant Brody Williams."

He'd never brought anyone from his personal life to work, but he wanted to show Mari. Tell her the truth and see how she handled it. If this didn't scare her, nothing would. But they were always honest with one another, and she had to see he had a darker side.

"Wow," she said as they arrived at the hangar. "They're so much bigger in person. You fly these?"

"All of them," he said, maybe a little proudly. "I'm teaching Viper navigation now, but I was flying a Stallion when—" His voice cut out and he cleared his throat.

"When you lost your friends in the crash," she said, finishing the sentence for him. She looped her arm around his and leaned into his shoulder. "I can't even imagine how tough that is for you. I've never experienced that kind of loss." He brought her around to face him and then he just hugged her. Hard.

"It's easier every day I'm around you, but I never forget. That's why I brought you here. I thought maybe I could make some new memories with the birds. Ones to help me through the tough times."

"You probably don't want to, and that's okay if that's the case, but if you do want to tell me about what happened, I, uh, I'll listen."

"That's why I brought you here. I want you to understand—" He wasn't sure what exactly. "Come on," he said. He took her hand and guided her through the bay door all the way to the cockpit. "Here. Sit down."

She glanced at her hands, which he noticed were trembling slightly. "I'm nervous, but not for me. For you. I know this is a big deal, Brody. I just don't want you to do anything that makes you feel worse or brings back the bad memories. You don't have to do this for me. After you explained on the yacht, I'm fine. Really."

She did understand better than most. That was how she was wired. She was kind and caring and that's why he had to tell her.

Dredging up the past was his least favorite thing to do, but something told him that he needed to do this. That she was the one person who would understand his hell. He focused on their hands holding tight to each other.

"We were heading back to base. The team had picked up some artillery from another base for transport. My guys had come along to do the heavy lifting. We were flying over some mountains in Afghanistan. It was just supposed to be a regular run, and then the rockets came out of nowhere. We were so heavy and I couldn't get her higher, and then I couldn't keep her up. We were only about three miles from base, but the rotors and fuel tanks were done. Whoever shot at us knew exactly what they were doing.

"The fire from the fuel took out everyone in the back, including my copilot when he tried to save the others, but then the whole bird blew apart. The next thing I knew I was on the ground with one of the blades coming for me. I ducked and rolled but it sliced across my back. You probably saw the scars. I broke ribs, an arm and a leg. Ruptured my spleen. But I survived. No one else did. The only reason I lived was because I was still in the front. It was sheer stupid luck. I shouldn't be here. I should be dead in that desert with my friends." His voice caught. He wasn't one for tears, but emotion clogged his throat.

"Brody," she choked and then sobbed. He glanced up to find tears streaming down her face.

"Babe, I'm sorry. I didn't mean to make you cry. I just wanted you to understand that I'm messed up. I lost so many who were close to me in one swoop. Those men were my brothers and they're gone. Just gone."

She stood and then slipped her arms around him. "I'm not crying because you told me, Brody. I'm crying because you were hurt. You could have died along with them. I wouldn't have ever known you. And that—it's selfish, but that makes me so sad. Now I can't imagine never knowing you. I care about you so much, and you've brought a lot to my life in such a short time. And I get why you're so torn up. You have every right to feel like that, but I'm grateful, Brody. So grateful that you're here and holding me."

Man, she was one of a kind. He kissed her. "New memories. This is why I wanted you here," he said as he squeezed her tight. "I've flown just about every bird except this one. But I want to do it, with you sitting right there." He pointed to the copilot's seat.

"Really. I've never even been in a helicopter. Won't you get in trouble with your boss? Taking it for personal use?"

He chuckled. "Technically, I'm about to take you on a training exercise. I have to fly a minimum amount each month and I'm a little low, especially with the Stallions. What do you think? Is this something you'd like to try?"

"If you're sure this is okay with you, I'm game

for anything, so long as you're next to me," she said. Her smile stretched across her face.

"I may take you up on that 'anything,' but first let's go for a ride. Hop up and I'll strap you in."

She clapped her hands. "I'm so excited. In a good way." He stepped across and made sure she was strapped in her seat. Then he put on the headphones. "You can talk to me through here." He pointed to the microphone attached to the headset. Then he double-checked her harness.

She gave him a winning smile.

He put on his headphones. "Are you ready?"

"Brody?"

"Yes?" He wondered if maybe it was a bit much for her. He'd just given her a lot to deal with—this was a big bird and for the uninitiated it could be intimidating. It was loud and a very different experience than flying in a commercial plane. He had grunts in his class who still cringed on liftoff.

"Thank you for making your new memories with me, and for sharing this."

It was Mari who was doing him the favor.

"There's no one I'd rather do this with. Let's go."

This was just one of many adventures he had planned for her.

New memories with Mari.

It was the first time he'd had a plan.

And the first time he'd been excited about living in almost a year.

12

FOR THE FIRST few minutes in the air, Mari was a nervous wreck. Her stomach churned and her hands gripped the sides of the seat. Then they flew out over the ocean and her heart slowed as the aircraft turned and hung in the air. She could see downtown Corpus clearly.

"You doing okay?" Brody asked.

She nodded and then remembered she needed to speak. "Yes," she replied. "It's so beautiful. I love it. As long as I don't look down, that is."

He chuckled. "You're doing great. Want to fly over your house, see what it looks like from up here?"

"That would be cool. But I'm also happy for you to do whatever it is you have to for the hours you have to get in."

"No worries. I mapped out our flight plan earlier. We're good."

He banked to the left and she soon recognized

some of the larger homes in the neighborhood before they reached their street. Everything appeared so organized and smaller down there. Unbelievable how much chaos was going on inside the house.

"It looks so peaceful," she said.

"That's one of the reasons I chose to live in the neighborhood. It was quiet. And I noticed when I stopped by for my interview that one of the neighbors was hot."

She turned to look at him. "What?"

He grinned, but kept his eyes straight ahead. "You were wearing a dark blue dress with cream-colored heels. I was sitting in the living room of the rental talking to the owner when I spotted you. I thought, dang, there is a *woman*."

He'd noticed her even then? "You're making that up."

"It was a Tuesday afternoon. You had your laptop bag, and that green tote thing you carry everywhere. You got out of the car, glanced at your phone and then you threw it across the yard. You had your eyes closed and your mouth went into a tight little line like it does when you're mad. You took off your shoes, traipsed across the yard to pick up your phone. Right then and there I wanted to know exactly what you were thinking. You seemed so prim and proper and I was curious about what made you angry."

He *had* seen her. She remembered that day and shook her head. "The ex texted and informed me he needed to pick up a few things from the house. He asked me to be gone during a certain time and I just lost it."

"Please tell me you didn't make it convenient for him."

She grinned. Now he would know she was crazy. "Well, I texted him back and told him he could basically forget it. That I'd gotten rid of his things the night he left me. I was lying through my teeth. The next weekend his things ended up at Goodwill. He had some pretty expensive suits in the pile and all these ties that he was so fussy about. Oh, and his stupid socks. He wore socks to bed because he didn't like touching feet. That should have been another big clue. That was when I found his other phone. And why did he need two? I'll tell you why, because he was a cheating jerk. Then I called his mom and told her what he did. Honestly, that's probably the most horrible thing I've ever done. It ruined her image of her perfect son. Later, he tried to tell her I was lying, but she knew. He'd brought whatever that woman's name is over for dinner. You met his mom, she's a lot smarter than he gives her credit for."

"I kind of love that you have a mean streak in you. Do you still have feelings for him?"

Wow. That had come out of the blue.

Brody still had a smile on his face, but it was strained. "Fact is, it's only been a few months."

"True. Let me think. Gosh…" She tapped her

finger on her chin for a second. "Um, nope. I meant what I said the other night. If it wasn't for him breaking up with me, I would have never known what I was missing. You've taught me so much about everything. I feel freer. When I was with that jerk, I was always a disappointment. I could never do anything right. I don't know why I put up with him. I guess I'm always a little too worried about what people think of me."

"Well, you're intelligent and sexy and…"

She sighed happily. "I feel the same way about you. I so want to strip you naked."

He laughed. "You can't say stuff like that while I'm flying. I have to concentrate."

He glanced over and she winked at him.

"Anything else you want to see from up here?"

"Oh, well, maybe where I have my office. I love that neighborhood, too. That's where I would have bought if my ex hadn't talked me into the fixer-upper that I knew I didn't have time for."

"Can you give me an idea of what part of town that is?"

That's right, they were in a helicopter. A giant one. She gave him a couple of landmarks to go by and a few minutes later they were hanging over the quaint little street that housed her office. She was proud of the place. It was a tiny craftsman that she and Abbott had overhauled. And it was paid for. It was one of the only reasons she hadn't gone under financially when she was stuck with the Victorian. They didn't have much overhead other than the utilities.

"I haven't been by there. That's really cute," he said.

"Thanks, Abbott and I are pretty proud of it."

"Time to head back to base. I have another surprise for you tonight."

"This has already been more than anyone could have wished for," she said. "Thank you again."

"Oh, we aren't done yet."

AN HOUR LATER Brody drove her to his favorite restaurant. The place was called Hildie's and it served German food. He'd reserved his favorite private table in the back, and they shared platters of perogies, spaetzle and schnitzel.

Her phone rang for the fifth time that night, but as usual she clicked it off.

"I don't mean to be nosy, but can I ask who's calling this late on a Sunday night?" From the wariness in his eyes, he was thinking it was a guy.

She didn't want to admit it, but she also didn't want him to think the worst. "My parents. It's the landline at their house. I love them, but they're a little overprotective sometimes. I keep texting them that I'm fine. Better than fine, actually, but they call anyway. They are not big on boundaries. I needed a little space after everything with Gary, but they don't seem to understand. And they're always coming at me with advice. If I tell them what's going on with the house, they'll want to step in and help."

"Would that be such a bad thing? You had it pretty rough there for a bit."

"Yeah, but it was my mess and I wanted to get myself out of it. Although, you did help me. But it was my idea to ask you for it. I still can't believe I did that."

"Honestly, it turned out pretty well for both of us."

Oh yeah, it did. When he smiled at her like he was right now, it did wonderful things to her body. And that was only his smile.

Since he seemed to be in the mood to talk, she thought he'd be willing to answer a few questions. She wanted to find out more about him. "I know your relationship with your dad is strained, but do you remember your mom?"

He nodded. "She smelled like roses, and she played games with me all the time. Every night after homework was done, we'd do hide-and-go-seek or a board game. My dad was different then. Like your parents, they were really happy together. When she died, I was just eleven and Dad and I were both lost. She'd been the biggest part of our lives. It was awful. It happened so fast. She found out she had a brain tumor and two weeks later she was dead."

"That's so sad. As much as my parents pester me, I can't imagine not having them in my life. And I have to admit, I haven't been the best of daughters lately. But they were kind of all up in my business about Gary, and then when he left I could feel their 'I told you so.' And there I've gone and made your sweet story about me again. Sorry."

"It's okay. I like hearing about your family. Are you and your sister close?"

"I thought we were. She's just as busy with work as I am. Always about to walk into a meeting. Maybe that's my karma. You know, I want to throw this big Valentine's Day party to sort of celebrate finishing the house. How would you feel if I invited your family and mine to the event? That way I can talk to them all at once, and show them how well I'm doing. I mean, I understand if you don't want to. Is that kind of strange, asking if you want to meet my parents?"

Why couldn't she just shut up?

"Nope, I'm already looking forward to it. I'm really curious about the people who raised you."

"Really?"

"Yeah, you're a sweetheart. They have to be good people."

That made her feel guilty. "They are."

Brody stared at his plate. The silence was broken when he told her, "We can invite my dad, but I can't promise he'll show up. I'd rather wait to introduce you to the stepsiblings. They can be a bit much, especially when they're all together at family gatherings."

"How do you feel about asking your boss?"

"We can do whatever you want. He asked about

your house the other day, so that might be a good idea. He knows a lot of people in town, he could maybe get you some clients."

Brody was always so thoughtful.

She took a bite of one of the perogies.

"These new jeans are not going to fit for very long if you keep feeding me like this," she said.

"Those jeans have been a part of a fantasy of mine since you opened the front door tonight."

The man was going to make her melt right in the middle of Hildie's. She wasn't sure what she'd done right to bring him into her life, but she was grateful it had happened.

HE LOVED HOW her cheeks turned pink when he complimented her. She really had no idea how attractive she was.

"Brody," she said and squeezed his arm. "Saying stuff like that makes me—"

"Hot?"

"Yes," she whispered. She blinked and her eyes looked a little out of focus. He kind of liked this game. That he could arouse her so quickly. He wondered if she had a clue as to how turned on he was. Even talking about family and parents hadn't doused the flames. He'd wanted her all night.

"Would you like to know what I'm going to do to you when we get home?"

She shook her head, but then she smiled.

"We're going to start in the kitchen. I have this fun little thing I want to do to you with ice cream."

She raised her hand at the waiter. "Check, please."

Brody chuckled and slid his fingers along her thigh. "Don't you want dessert?"

"I thought I was dessert," she said. That twinkle of mischief in her eyes pulled at him. His body tensed with need.

"We have to add some whipped cream to that kitchen fantasy," he said, teasing her.

"And champagne. I want to pour it all over you and lick it off," she whispered and then nibbled his ear.

His jeans were way too tight, and his hand squeezed her thigh. "We may have to start by christening the truck," he said. "I'm not sure I'm going to make it to the house."

He paid the check and they were out of there in a matter of minutes.

If the parking lot hadn't been so well lit directly in front of the restaurant, he would have taken her right then. But he'd held it together until they were inside her front door.

Just as he promised, he led her toward the kitchen. "Finally. I've wanted to do this all day," he said as he leaned in and kissed her. His fingers tightened in her hair as he teased her mouth open. Something had changed between them. This felt new. Stronger. More potent. At his very core, he needed her and had to have her.

She captured his tongue with her own. Stroked it. He loved it when she did that. It reminded him of her mouth on his cock. A minute passed, maybe two before she stepped back and tugged him over to the oak table. "You promised we'd start here, Marine." She posed sexy for a moment, and then began clearing a space on the brand-new table. "Jeans off or on?" she asked when she turned to face him.

His eyebrows shot up. She had no idea of the extent of her powers. He was impressed by her boldness. In the last few weeks, she'd begun to trust herself and it was one of the sexiest things about her. That and her luscious body and that cute smile. That smile did him in every time.

"Off," he said. He put his hands on his waist as he waited for the show to begin.

She unzipped the jeans, but stopped. "I'm not sure you're ready for what you're about to see," she warned. She pulled back one side of the zipper to show a flash of red silk. "I was planning to wear these on Valentine's Day, but I thought, since Brody has a surprise or two in store for me, maybe I'll give him one in return." She kicked off her sneakers and then slid the jeans down.

He hissed in a breath and started toward her, but she held out a hand. "Wait, you haven't seen the best part." The room was almost dark, so she switched on the makeshift lamp in the corner. The soft light bathed her in gold.

Slowly, she turned and bent over the table, and the breath he'd been holding came out in a whoosh.

His name was tattooed across her panties. "Brody" was stitched on the red silk covering her ass.

Something dark and possessive rose up in him.

"When did you buy those?"

"Today. The lingerie shop does it as a novelty. I was kind of hoping you'd like it. I didn't want you to take it the wrong way."

"I love it," he said.

He was already unbuttoning his jeans as he crossed the floor. Pressing into her, his hands caressed her butt. And then he pulled the silk down to her ankles. She stepped out of the panties, and he stuffed them in his pocket. "I'm keeping these," he growled.

She glanced behind her and winked at him. "It's okay, I had seven pairs made. So six more days to go." The image of her wearing his name across her backside every day pushed him to the edge. That happened a lot with her, his losing control.

It made him laugh to realize how tightly wound he'd been when he'd met her. In fact, he didn't think he'd ever been this relaxed or open with anyone. It only made him want her more.

"Bend over."

"Bossy," she said cheekily, but did so.

He ran his hand over her and sucked in a quick breath. "You're wet for me."

She chuckled. "I have been since I watched you

fly that helicopter. Seeing you so determined, so raw, Brody, it almost made me come while we were in the air."

She was trying to kill him. Seriously trying to kill him. No way would he have been able to keep his focus on flying if that had happened. But the fantasy of it made him even harder.

He teased her clit again and her back arched. He wanted to please her; he would please her. In mere seconds she was breathing hard, calling out his name. "Tell me what you want, Mari," he asked. He would do it, he'd do anything she wanted.

"You, please. Inside me. I need you, Brody."

Sweeter words had never been spoken he thought.

After sliding on a condom, he tested her opening. She was still so tight. In some way—all right, in many ways—it was as if this gorgeous woman had been made for him. In every way, she was what he needed—and what he desired.

"Brody, please." She pressed back against his erection.

Having vowed to please her, he could wait no longer.

He eased himself into her and then let her set the tempo. His hand curved along her hip. Keeping the rhythm going with his cock, he reached around and touched her slick heat. Her breath hitched and she did that little humming thing that told him she was almost there. Good thing, since he wasn't far behind.

She mewled and increased the pace. He quickly went to hold onto her hips, whispering every bit of encouragement he could think of. "Is this what you wanted when you were flying with me?" He thrust into her, whispering into her ear, "What we're doing right now? Come for me, Mari."

"Yes," she cried. "Oh, yes." She arched her back, gripping the table hard as she climaxed.

"Babe," he murmured, surrendering himself to the same sensation, to the staggering emotions he felt for her. This was what it meant to be consumed by someone. That's what Mari had done to him.

It scared him, and yet at the same time he realized he was pleased.

Really pleased.

MARI STOOD STARING at herself in the bathroom mirror. She felt branded by Brody. There wasn't an inch of her body he hadn't kissed, stroked or known intimately in the last few hours, and she loved it. He'd made an ice cream sundae out of her in the kitchen. Now every time she was in the kitchen she'd remember his mouth on her, teasing her, making love to her.

It was magical. And scary. She might have thought she was in love with her ex, but now she knew what it really meant to be in love. What she had with Brody went far beyond the sex. This connection they had, it was what her parents had. And while he didn't seem in any hurry to end their arrangement, she felt as if she needed to put some kind of locked cage around her heart.

It had to be coming. She didn't get to be this happy. And she was. For the first time in a long time, she was well and truly happy. A few days ago she'd promised herself that she'd enjoy every moment she had with him. Fear would not be a part of this equation.

But that didn't keep her from speculating about the end of whatever this glorious thing was between them.

She walked from the bathroom back into the bedroom and pulled one of his clean T-shirts over her head. He'd left a few in her dresser for when they finished work and showered or bathed together. Almost every night they spent it here. Another place where the memories would be strong.

He was sound asleep. She had to confess she was a little nervous. They were having an actual sleepover. It had also been his first flight in the big helicopter since his accident. Would he have one of his nightmares?

Before they'd gone upstairs to clean off after their sundae making, she'd seen him chug a couple of pills along with a bottle of water. She was worried he was getting one of his headaches, so in the shower she'd shampooed him, washed him and then shooed him out, telling him that she needed time to recuperate.

Now what do I do.

After the awful stories that he'd shared with her, she was worried for him. She tried not to be afraid that he'd lash out while he slept, but they'd flown for some time in the same kind of helicopter he'd been shot down in.

Did she join him in the bed and risk waking him? Or go downstairs and sleep on the couch, and risk offending him? He was trying so hard to make this work.

"Are you going to stand there and stare at me all night, or are you coming to bed?"

She squeaked and then laughed. He pulled the comforter down for her to slide in beside him. "I just had this dream about the sexiest woman I've ever seen, climbing into bed with me. Is that my T-shirt?"

"Yes."

"It looks way better on you."

She wasn't so sure about that.

He pulled her in close to him and she draped one leg over his thigh. "I'm nervous about falling asleep," he said. "But you've worn me out. I don't think I could move even if I wanted to."

She kissed his jaw. It was rough with stubble but she loved it.

"If I hear you make a noise, I promise to get out of bed as fast as I can. I'm nervous for you, too. I don't want you to feel bad if you can't go to sleep. It won't hurt my feelings if you need to go home. I mean it."

"I was serious. I don't want to move an inch right now," he said against her hair. "I love smelling you as I close my eyes." He yawned.

"Go to sleep." She snuggled into him. "We have a lot more rooms to christen tomorrow. You need your beauty rest."

"You're beautiful enough for the both of us," he whispered.

When he said things like that, her pulse raced and her heart beat triple time in her chest. It was all she could do not to climb back on top of him and make love to him for another couple of hours. But she resisted. The guy deserved a break after the phenomenal memories they'd created tonight.

His loving her was honestly one of the highlights of her life.

It wasn't long before his breathing evened out and his muscles relaxed. She allowed herself to close her eyes.

Yes, this is what she wanted. A man who believed in her and thought she was beautiful, one who was consumed with bringing her pleasure. A man who was everything she ever dreamed of for a partner and then some.

No, she wouldn't let fear steal whatever time she had left with him. At least not yet. She'd keep him for as long as he wanted to be here. Maybe that wouldn't be forever, but for now they were in a good place.

"Mari?" She smiled. She thought he'd gone to sleep.

"You okay?" she asked.

"Tonight was one of the best nights of my life. I just wanted you to know that. And there's no place I'd rather be right now. No place."

Her heart soared. "Me, too."

13

"I MIGHT THROW UP," Mari said as she straightened the silverware on the table for the fifth time in an hour. Everything was ready. She'd planned her Valentine's Day dinner party down to the last candied mint. And she'd invited a ton of people. From Brody's CO to potential clients, she even invited her parents from Austin and his dad.

She and Brody were making new memories. And she hoped maybe she could help him with his past disappointments. His dad had said he wasn't sure he could come, but he would try. He was working in Dallas, which was a pretty short flight.

Half of her hoped the man showed up, the other half hoped he didn't. She wasn't sure what she'd say to him. Though she was glad Brody hadn't minded her meddling.

He slipped his arms around her from behind and pulled her in close. "You're perfect. Everything looks great. The house is a showplace. They're all going to be impressed." He kissed her neck. Oh, how she lived for those touches.

For the past few days Brody had been extrasensitive while helping her. He'd seen her crazy side and survived. She'd bark orders, he'd give her the sexiest of smiles and do whatever she asked. Then at night he'd take her to bed and they'd make love. He told her that he craved her, that she was wreaking havoc on his sanity. That he couldn't stop thinking about her.

And she felt the same way about him. They weren't burning out, they were burning hotter.

Meanwhile, she could finally sell the money pit. Be out from under the horrific weight of debt she felt. Except she'd worked so hard on it she had mixed feelings. Seeing it going to someone else would break her heart. This was the house she'd created with Brody.

They'd had so much fun and there were so many wonderful memories. She hoped tonight would show him that they had what it took. She could let him see how happy her parents were and that some lucky relationships did last. She wanted that with Brody. Smiling, she knew she was ready to share her heart, and that Brody was a man worthy of it.

He squeezed her tight. "Everyone who is coming tonight loves you. Don't be nervous."

She turned and put her hands on his chest. "I can't wait for you to meet my mom and dad. They're disgustingly joyful together. I'm really curious about these surprise guests they're bringing."

"I wish I could say I was joyful about you meeting my dad. There's a good chance the guest he's bringing is someone he met last night in a bar or restaurant. Don't let it ruin your night. Just say the word and I'll ask him to go."

She kissed him. "It's okay. Not to worry. He spawned you, so he can't be all bad."

"In case I forget to say it later, you're exceptional. And this spread is exceptional, too." He pointed at the variety of food on the table. The rest was waiting in the fridge.

"Oh, I almost forgot the roast. I need to get it out of the oven." She pulled away and hustled into the kitchen. That's when it dawned on her. There was no smell of meat cooking.

No. No. No.

She yanked open the door and gasped. The raw meat sat in the roasting pan.

She slammed the door shut and turned the oven temperature up to 500 degrees. She'd cook it on high for a bit, and then lower it after about forty-five minutes. If she basted it with broth, it wouldn't dry out too much. They were doing a buffet since there were so many invited, and the roast was only one of many dishes. Still, it was Brody's favorite and she wanted it on the menu. This party was for both of them.

"What's wrong?" Brody asked. Lately, he'd always been there for her. Last minute touch-up painting or shopping, whatever she needed. No man had ever been such a willing partner with her, and she loved it. Loved every second of it.

"Been so distracted running around at the last minute that I forgot to turn on the oven. So dinner may be delayed a bit. Luckily, we have other things to eat. And my parents are always late, so there's that. They'll be the excuse to wait on dinner. It'll be fine," she said as she tried to convince herself.

"I can order something from one of the local restaurants if you're worried."

She laughed. "It's Valentine's Day. By the time it would be ready and get here, the roast will be done." She took a deep breath. "It's okay. Something always goes wrong." Of course, that meant her warming times for the rest of the food were also messed up.

"I may have to use the oven at your house to reheat the twice mashed potatoes."

"Whatever you need," he said.

"Thank you. For being here," she said as she made her way around the marble-topped island. "It's going to be okay, right?"

"Yes." He brushed a curl from her cheek and kissed her. "Do you think we have time for a quick run upstairs?"

She frowned. "No."

"It might help with your nerves."

There was that. "Hmm. Maybe—"

The doorbell rang. "Who could that be?"

"The party doesn't start for an hour," Brody said as he glanced behind him. "Did you order anything?"

She shook her head and walked past him. The flowers and baked goods had been delivered earlier in the day.

Peeking through the security peephole Brody had insisted they put in, she frowned. Again.

She opened the door. "Mom, Dad? You guys are early."

Her mother gave her a nervous smile. "Hi, honey. We wanted to see the house before everyone got here." Her mom leaned in and kissed her cheek.

"Oh, wonderful." Her parents were notoriously late to everything. Something was up.

Her dad thrust a giant bouquet of flowers toward her and then kissed her other cheek. "Yes. See the house, and there's something we need to talk to you about."

"Okay, well come in. I have someone I want to introduce you to." She stepped back and noticed a couple behind them. "Hi, you must be Mom and Dad's friends." She smiled.

It was unusual that her parents had invited friends, but then this party was for everyone who didn't have a place to go on Valentine's Day. It was such a weird holiday and extremely lonely for many people. So Mari had adopted a more-is-merrier attitude.

The elegant woman was familiar, but it took Mari a moment to place her. "Mrs. Sangle?"

"Hello, Mari. Your home is beautiful," she said as she stepped over the threshold. Mrs. Sangle had lived down the street from her family for as long as she could remember. Her husband had died last year, and Mom and Dad had been looking out for her.

"Thank you. It's good to see you," she said.

The man next to Mrs. Sangle held out his hand. "Hi, I'm Joe Heely. I'm a…friend."

"Nice to meet you." She gestured for him to come inside. He was tall with thick white hair. He seemed very distinguished.

"I'm so glad you're all here. This is my friend, Lieutenant Brody Williams." She knew she was grinning like a silly schoolgirl as she introduced him. "He's been helping me with the house. I could not have finished it without him."

They all shook hands, and then there was an awkward silence. "Let's go into the family room. It's at the back of the house. It's larger than these front rooms, so I thought it'd be best for us to hang out there until dinner."

"Um," her mother said. "That's great, honey. Is there a place that your father and I can speak to you privately? Just for a few minutes?"

They glanced at one another nervously. What the heck was going on? She'd never seen them act like this before.

"Sure. Brody, can you take Mr. Heely and Mrs. Sangle back to the kitchen? Get them a drink. And the cold appetizers are on the second shelf, if you could go ahead and set those out." She handed him the flowers her dad had given her. "And there's a glass vase in the china cabinet that will work for these. You can just put them on the breakfast bar."

"Got it," he said as he gave her a quick smile. "Folks, follow me."

He led them down the hallway. Her parents stayed behind. "What's going on?" she said quickly.

"Is there some place with a door?" her mother asked. What an odd request.

"My office?" She motioned for them to follow her. Now she was really nervous. Was one of them ill? Tears sprang to her eyes, but she blinked them away. She wouldn't borrow trouble.

Mari leaned on the edge of the desk and her parents sat on the sofa.

"We've been trying to get in touch with you for several months," her mother said. "But you've been so busy we haven't managed more than a three- or four-minute conversation."

Mari blew out a breath. They were going to lecture her about being a bad daughter. She deserved it.

"Yeah. Sorry. After the breakup, I just needed some time. You guys always seem to have it so together in the relationship department. It's tough when I can't seem to get it right."

"We're divorced," her father blurted.

Mari's hand slipped off the desk and if she hadn't been perched on the edge she would have fallen. "What?" she squeaked.

"Last year, actually. Very amicable," her mother said. She grabbed her father's hand. "We're still the best of friends and love each other dearly. But we haven't been in love for a long time."

This was some weird nightmare. A. Horrible. Horrible. Nightmare.

Wake up, Mari.

"I can see this is a bit of a shock," her father said. "We didn't want to spring it on you tonight, but there was never a good time. And we've been with our new partners for a while now, and we wanted them to meet you."

Her parents were divorced. How did this happen? She'd spent her entire life admiring their deep love. And here they weren't in love anymore.

She sniffed. "But if you love each other, you make it work," she said on a whisper. "You always told me that."

"We had, we still have a wonderful relationship based on trust and friendship. But for the last twenty years or so, neither of us has had the passion for one another that one should in a marriage," her mother said.

"Passion isn't what makes a marriage. How many times did you tell me that? When I came to you for advice and you said that a solid foundation isn't built on passion alone." Anger boiled deep in her gut. They'd lied to her. All of these years they hadn't been happy. Her whole life had been a lie.

"It isn't the main ingredient for a successful relationship," her dad said, "but it is a necessary one. For happiness, you need to be passionate about that other person."

Her parents were talking about passion? "Wrong. Wrong. Wrong. I refuse to accept this. You two need to work it out. All marriages go through tough times. You told me that, too. You've never had a rough patch. Ever. And at the first hint of…maybe one of you is going through some kind of midlife crisis you just give up." Her voice rose. Never had she been this upset at her parents. Not even when they refused to let her date when she was sixteen. Not even when they refused to let her go to an out-of-state college even though she had a scholarship.

They'd always been protective and loving, sometimes to a fault. And now this. "What the hell is wrong with you?"

"Mari, watch your language," her mother said.

"Watch my language! I'm not twelve, Mom. You can't tell me to watch my language when you guys have been lying to me for this long. And now you're saying that your marriage was a sham? Really? Which means you've been lying for years!"

"Screaming never helps anything," her mom said. "And our marriage wasn't a sham. We've been talking about this and we didn't see the sense in hurting you and your sister, or breaking up the family unless we each found someone else. But we didn't."

"At least, not until last year. Your mom met Joe at one of her art classes. And Janet and I have been growing closer since her husband died. We decided that before we did something we would regret, we'd go ahead and divorce."

"Wait, so does Daisy know yet?" Her sister would have called her surely. No way she knew.

Her parents glanced at her. "Well, she was our mediator for the divorce. We asked her not to say anything to you until we had a chance to talk to you in person."

And they'd chosen tonight.

Oh, my god. My parents brought dates to my party.

"Those people out there? You introduced them to me—tonight? What is wrong with you? Do you have any idea how important this was for me? I can't believe you've done this on the one night when I needed you."

Mari twisted her hair around her finger. Disaster. "Listen to me. I have very important people coming tonight. Clients I'm trying to impress. You're not ruining this for me. You will go out there and pretend to be happy. You'll be the old you. Not these people I don't understand at all. If you ever loved me, you'll send those people home that you brought with you. I mean it."

She stormed out and slammed the door.

The doorbell rang.

Not now. She pasted on her everything-is-perfect face and met Brody at the front door.

"You okay? I heard yelling." He was so sweet. Tears threatened again. "Mari? Babe, what happened?"

She shook her head. She was going to show him what a wonderful loving relationship her parents had. What a joke. She sniffed and blinked several times. "I will be fine." After taking a deep breath, she let it out slowly. "Let's just get through this."

She opened the door.

"Mr. and Mrs. Harker, so good to see you." Mari introduced the couple to Brody. "This is the couple I was telling you about. They want a redesign of their kitchen and dining area."

Brody shook hands and hung Mrs. Harker's jacket in the hall closet. The doorbell rang again. The handsome man on the doorstep had to be Brody's dad. He was an older version of the man she so cared about.

She held out her hand and shook his. "It's nice to meet you, I'm Mari."

"Ah, so you're Mari. No wonder my son is so enamored. You're a looker."

"Dad," Brody interrupted. "Stop hitting on my girlfriend." He put a protective arm around her.

His girlfriend. Nerves fluttered around her belly. She'd waited weeks for him to mean that. But she wasn't sure he did now. It might still be an act.

His CO was coming up the drive and Brody might have said it in case the other man heard.

After her parents' admission, she wasn't sure who she could trust anymore.

You only have to get through the next couple of hours. Hang in there.

"Dad, I'd like you to meet Commander Gray, who runs the base I work on." He motioned to the CO. The two men exchanged handshakes.

"Mari, you look so pretty, and this house has come a long way from the photos you showed me at my birthday party," Gray said.

"Thanks. I couldn't have done any of it without Brody's help. He's a man who gets the job done fast."

The CO nodded. "Yes, he is. One of the best I have on base."

Mari glanced up to see Brody's eyebrows draw together. The CO just paid him a compliment, he should have been happy.

"Brody, can—" She'd started to ask him to take them to join the other guests when an alarm suddenly screeched.

They stared at each other for a second before they took off running for the kitchen. Smoke billowed out of the oven.

Brody grabbed the extinguisher from the pantry. "Get back," he ordered as she tossed him the hot pads she pulled from the nearest drawer. He used one to open the oven door and then sprayed inside.

White foam flew all over the kitchen as the smoke continued to billow. She ran and opened the back door. "Everyone on the patio until the smoke clears," she said to the guests. "Dad, do me a favor and start a fire in the pit in the backyard to keep people warm. Better a fire out there than in here," she said, trying to joke about the situation. Mortified didn't begin to describe the sinking sensation in the pit of her stomach.

"Tell me what I can do to help," Commander Gray asked.

"Get a broom from the closet and use the handle to punch the reset button on the alarm, please," Mari asked, barely keeping it together. "Mom, I need you to open all the windows."

People rushed to do what she'd asked. Mari swallowed over the frog in her throat.

"Sorry, folks. Technical difficulties," Brody said as he pulled the burned roast out of the oven. He started laughing. "I've had blackened fish and seafood, but never roast."

And that was it. The last straw. It just hit her wrong. She couldn't take it anymore.

"How can you laugh?" Even though she was being foolish, she couldn't stop. This wasn't his fault. "I mean, really? Now you have to decide to be a jerk?" For someone who never yelled, she was doing a lot of it tonight. But there was no stopping her tirade. Anger roiled through her body. "Everything is ruined. I wanted one special night. One.

This would have been the first time that Valentine's Day would have actually meant something to me. The first time I was going to share it with you. And then you laugh when you know how important this is to me."

"Mari, I'm sorry." Brody moved toward her, his face tense. She was a terrible person. "Tell me what else is wrong."

For a moment she let his arms wrap around her and she leaned into him. Then she remembered his CO was still standing there. Was it an act? And how would she ever know? Were there no more honest people in the world?

Tonight was a complete and utter failure and it hadn't even begun.

She couldn't breathe and it had nothing to do with the smoke that had filled the room. Backing away, she shook her head. "I have to get out of here," she said. When she turned, her parents stood there with worried looks.

"Leave. Go back to your lives, whoever you're spending them with. I can't believe this has happened"

"Mari, wait," Brody called after her.

She sped through the house and threw open the front door only to slam into a wall of a man.

Chin lifted, she found herself in the arms of Brody's friend Ben, and he was with Carissa. "Of course it's you. Because what else could happen to make this nightmare worse than for *you* to show up right now."

"What's that smell?" Carissa asked, making a face.

"Carissa," Ben said, "it's obvious Mari's upset. Are you okay?"

Mari was about to lose it, although she'd done enough damage by being rude. "Please," she said through gritted teeth. "Enjoy the appetizers. Everyone is out on the patio."

She hurried past them and started walking down the block.

"Mari!" Brody's tone was sharp. "Stop. Where are you going?"

In a fraction of a second he'd caught up to her. "I need a minute, okay? I'm sorry I yelled. I know that doesn't make it right, but I am sorry. You can't fix what's wrong right now. If you care about me at all, you'll leave me alone. You'll go back in there and make sure people have fun and see the great work we did on the place, okay?"

"I'm sorry about the roast. I shouldn't have laughed."

He thought this was because he'd laughed. She closed her eyes and took another deep breath. "I'm not mad at you, Brody. I swear. I had some upsetting news from my parents and I'm not dealing with it very well. It just… I don't know what I believe anymore. Who I trust. I don't know anything."

Tears spilled down her cheeks. "It's funny, two hours ago I thought I finally had done something right. That's what I get for being cocky. I had you, the house in good shape. And the party was going to be my chance to show everyone that I finally had it together.

"But I don't. I never will. I don't even know if you're a real boyfriend or still the guy I just have sex with. How sad is that?"

"Mari, you know I care about you."

"That's what I'm trying to explain to you. I don't know that. I know we have fantastic sex and we get along, but do you love me? I do love you. But even now, I can't be sure if you hugged me in there because you cared, or because your boss was watching."

"Mari! How could you even think that?"

She let the tears flow. "I told you in the beginning I was a mess. Listen, if you care about me, if you ever did or do, please go back in and try and entertain them. Or just send them all home. I don't care anymore."

Then she started walking again.

She had no idea where she was going, but she had to get away.

Far, far away.

14

IT TOOK EVERYTHING Brody had to leave her and return to the house. That's what she wanted, and that's what he'd do. But her words shredded him. He'd tried the last two weeks to show her how important she was to him. He'd shared his demons, and she'd made him whole.

And yet she still doubted if what they had was real. What was he supposed to do with that? What else could he do to prove to her that she made him think about them being more than temporary lovers.

Where the hell was she? The smoke was gone, and it had been a good thirty minutes with no sign of Mari. If she didn't come back soon, he'd go out and search for her.

Her mother had helped him get the rest of the appetizers heated in the microwave and they'd put the potatoes in the oven at his house. From Nikki's Italian Bistro, he ordered chicken marsala and a veggie pasta dish just in case someone didn't eat meat. The owner had become friends with Brody since he visited the cozy family restaurant at least once a week.

"Everything okay?" Mari's father asked. He'd been making sure they all had drinks. Brody nodded. After the initial excitement over the smoke, everyone had pretty much laughed it off. They were all talking, nibbling and mingling. It had become a proper party.

Except the hostess was MIA. What had happened with her parents? She'd been fine before that.

He glanced around. Things seemed to be under control for the moment.

Even his dad was behaving. He'd come without a date. There was a first time for everything.

There was something going on with his dad. Something in his eyes, sadness. Except for the two years right after Brody's mother died, his dad had always been the life of the party. But throughout the evening, Brody had seen him standing outside, staring up at the stars.

"I'm worried about her," Mari's mother said quietly to her father. "You should go look for her. It's been a rough night."

"I doubt she wants to talk to either one of us," her father said. The man approached him. "Brody, would you mind seeing if you can find her? We, uh, probably aren't her favorite people right now."

Brody set aside the salad he'd been preparing at

the counter. That was one of the many things Mari had taught him in the last week. He could make a mean salad. "What were you all talking about? She has you two on a pedestal."

"Not anymore," her mother said. "I'm afraid we are well and truly knocked off that."

"Permanently. We should have held off tonight," he said. "She was right about that. It was stupid."

"Tell her what?" Brody was confused. Was one of them not well? That would explain her stress.

"We got a divorce and didn't tell her." Her father set his beer on the counter. "We've been trying to talk to her for the last three months, but she either wouldn't take our calls or she'd hang up before we could get to discuss it."

Divorced?

That would have crushed her. She idolized their relationship. He really felt for her. No wonder she'd reacted the way she had.

"And you picked tonight?"

"Yes, in hindsight not our brightest move. But we've been trying to tell her—"

Brody took off, only pausing to stop by the family room. "Sir, can I talk to you for a minute?"

The CO followed him out to the hallway.

"What's up, Lieutenant?"

"I need a favor, sir. I've found out Mari's had some really bad personal news on top of the burned dinner. I need to go find her. I was wondering if you and Carissa could keep an ear out for the delivery man. And get everyone set up in the dining room."

"Got it. Do what you have to, Marine. Let us know if we need to form a search party."

Hell, he hadn't thought about that. What if she'd taken off and he couldn't find her. "Thank you, sir. Hopefully, we'll be back shortly."

Just as he reached the foyer he saw Mari sneaking upstairs. Thankfully, she was okay. He never should have walked away from her earlier, despite what she'd said.

He followed her.

She went into the master bedroom and closed the door. She probably needed a minute to freshen up.

He waited on the top step, but when she didn't come out, he decided to go in.

She sat on the edge of the bed, her hands wrapped around her middle. "Hey," he said, and sat down beside her.

"Hey," she whispered.

"Been a challenge these last few hours."

"You could say that. Are they gone?"

"I think you know they aren't. They're concerned for you. And no one is more worried about you than I am." He started to put an arm around her, but she jumped up and moved across the room.

"Talk to me," he said.

"I don't want to, Brody. I'm sorry. But I need you to go. I just need everyone to go away."

"Mari, be reasonable." He tried to reach for her, but she pulled away.

"Reasonable? Oh, that's exactly what I'm being. You don't get it. I know how this works out. What happened downstairs—that's how it ends. There are no fairy tales or happy endings. Not real ones. Love comes and goes. If my parents couldn't make it work, no one can. Especially not a damaged commitment-phobe and the hot mess that I am."

His heart ached for her but he didn't know what to say. "Mari, you had a bad night. I can't even imagine what you're feeling right now."

"You're correct on both counts," she said.

"Tell me what you need." He spoke the words and at the same time was afraid of what she might say.

"I need you to get those people downstairs out of my house, and then I need to be alone. Thank you. For everything. You went above and beyond these last few weeks, but you and I both know this was temporary between us. The house is done. Time for each of us to move on."

A punch in the gut would have been easier to take. She'd made him consider a future for them. And now he couldn't see his future without her, but here she was ready to move on?

"Mari, think about what you're saying."

She rubbed her tears away. "I am. It was all-consuming, this thing with you. I've never— It woke me up. You made me realize I never want to settle again."

"And being with me is settling?"

"No. You're pretty much *everything*. But it will never work with us. You can't handle long-term. Do you honestly see yourself as the serious-commitment type? Look at your dad's track record. I'm giving you an out. Take it. Please. I'm begging you. I may not be strong enough to walk away if this goes on for much longer. I need you to go. I need us to leave on good terms. Otherwise, eventually you'll decide you can't handle it—and that will break me."

No words came to him. He did think about a forever with Mari, but he couldn't predict the future. Maybe he was like his dad. He cared about Mari, never cared about anyone more, but could he promise they'd last?

Was she right? It didn't feel like it. Leaving her felt wrong. The worst idea ever. But maybe they both needed a little time.

He leaned in and kissed her forehead. "I would do anything for you. You're upset right now. You need to cool down. I'm not going to ask them to leave right now. The ones who don't know what's going on are having a good time. And you have clients down there. Shoving them out the door won't look so great for your business. I'll tell them you have a headache. You stay up here." He headed for the door.

"Brody?"

"Yeah."

"I'm sorry. I'm grateful to you for everything, but I meant what I said. We promised to be honest with one another, right? This is me being honest. I need tonight to be it. I need you to be the strong one. I need you to walk away."

The strong one? She'd cut him to pieces. Unable to speak, he nodded, turned and left.

Good thing that Marines didn't cry, at least as far as he knew.

Brody fixed a smile on his face and went downstairs.

He wasn't sure how he made it through the makeshift dinner. Or talked to her clients about how talented and wonderful she was. While on the inside, he was a mess. Once dinner was over, people started leaving.

He showed her potential clients the whole house, except for the master. Explained how she'd gone to great lengths to make sure the place was restored correctly and at the same time had incorporated modern amenities.

They'd been impressed. Two of the couples had asked that she call them when she was feeling better. He promised to pass along their messages.

He shut the door behind the last of them, and then sighed with relief, grateful he no longer had to pretend.

"Let us help you finish cleaning up," Mari's mother said. He knew Mari wouldn't be happy about her parents still being in the house. They were the reason she'd spiraled out of control. Brody knew what that felt like, he was headed that way himself.

"No. I've got it," he said, ushering them to the door. They left reluctantly. Only his own dad remained.

"Son, you've had a busy night."

"Yep," Brody said. He just wanted his dad to go.

"There's something we need to talk about, but it can wait until tomorrow."

He remembered the sadness in his dad's eyes when he'd arrived. "Found a new lady tonight?" If his dad had something to say that was usually it.

His dad gave him a weak smile. "I deserve that. No, but like I said, it can wait."

"Tell me now."

"I have cancer."

Well, hell. That he didn't see coming.

More than an hour later, he'd sent his dad to his house to get some rest.

Then Brody stood at the base of the stairs and folded his arms. It had been an unpredictable night for both of them. More than anything he wanted to talk to her about what had happened with his dad. She was the first person he'd thought of to speak to, to confide in.

But she'd been through a lot. He had to try and make her see that she was wrong about them. And she was. The more he thought about it, the more he realized that this was no temporary fling. His feelings for her were so strong.

He'd clean up and give her time to get herself together.

Then he'd tell her that she'd made a mistake.

But what if she wasn't wrong? He loaded the dishwasher and took out the trash. Her mom had cleared off the table and put most of the food away before she'd gone.

Her parents had the perfect relationship. She'd told him that over and over again. And yet, they were divorced. And they were already with other people after nearly thirty years of marriage.

Maybe she had a point.

Had he changed? Sure she made him think about tomorrow and the next day. But he'd never been that kind of guy before. What made him one now?

Would he eventually get bored and break her heart?

That didn't feel right. But then what did he know about feelings?

Walk away.

No, he needed to run, and then maybe punch something.

15

IN THE WEE hours of the morning, a disheveled Mari ventured downstairs to find it dark. She pushed back the curtains to let in the early light.

The smoky smell was gone, and the place was immaculate. It was as if no one had ever been there. Brody must have cleaned up before he left.

What kind of guy did that after what she'd done? She'd been a complete jerk to him. Given him orders to get rid of her guests and then told him to get lost.

Yep. Mari the winner strikes again.

But hadn't she done them both a favor? Sure they were hot for one another, but that would obviously peter out.

Look at her parents.

She remembered when she was a kid being embarrassed because they were always kissing and hugging.

All of her memories, especially of their family holidays, were of her parents making everything fun and wonderful. Their little loving family going on grand adventures. They'd provided her and her sister, Daisy, an idyllic life. And now she felt as if all of that was a fraud. She'd been unaware that her parents were only together for their girls.

So wrong.

She pulled one of the open bottles of wine from the fridge and then found a glass. After pouring herself half the bottle, she sat down on a stool. There was a piece of paper under the whimsical cookie jar she'd set on the counter.

Hey,

Sorry you had such a bad night. I had a chance to take the Harkers and the Smiths through the rest of the house. They loved it. They asked that you give them a call when you feel better.

You helped me find my heart again, and I'll be forever grateful to you. I know you're hurting, but I hope that some day you can find forgiveness for your parents. What they did was wrong, but you never know how much time you have with people. It's important to make the most of it. You taught me that as well.

You are an amazing human being. I wish you the best, Mari. You deserve it.

B

Oh, no. The tears began again. *What have I done?* After everything, he'd tried to save future jobs for her. Done his level best to see out the rest of her party the way she'd wanted it. He was so kind and generous, someone she could trust. And she'd thrown it all away—everything they'd been building for the last month with a few harsh words.

I wish you the best.

It sounded so final. So *very* final.

As if it had been easy for him to walk away. Maybe she hadn't been so wrong after all.

Maybe she'd acted her worst, and he'd decided it wasn't such a bad idea to bail. Who could blame him? She should apologize. But then what?

"Hey."

Mari screamed. She bolted from her seat and turned to find Daisy standing there in her pajamas. "Daisy, you scared the crap out of me. What are you doing here?"

Her sister shrugged. "Where are the glasses?"

Mari pointed to the cabinet. After choosing one and pouring herself some wine, Daisy sat on the bar stool next to her.

"What's wrong?" Daisy asked, but she had a feeling her sister knew the answer.

"Everything."

"Sorry I showed up late. My flight was delayed. I…actually, I almost stayed home, but I knew they were coming and—"

"That they'd tell me something either they or you

should have told me a while ago?" She wanted to be mad but she couldn't be.

"I've wanted to, so many times. I needed you, Mari. It's been the worst. We idolized them. Thought they…well, you know. It devastated me. Probably the same as you're feeling right now."

"Impossible. I can't believe you really couldn't find the time to tell me."

"It was tough. I picked up the phone a dozen times. And the one time I tried was the night you called and told me about Gary…" Daisy paused. "I couldn't put more grief on you. And you're always busy. Before that you were trying to keep your business going, and you and your ex were buying this house. Then you wouldn't answer your phone at all. I got the occasional text. You did the same thing to Mom and Dad. That's no excuse for what they did last night, but they did try to talk to you."

She thought about how often she'd ignored the calls from her family. She sighed.

"I don't know up from down anymore," Mari said. "If they can't make it, what hope do the rest of us have?"

"Yep. But these new people they're dating. They're really into them."

Mari massaged her temples. "I can't get my head around it."

"If it makes you feel better, I've known longer than you have and I still have a tough time with it."

"No. That doesn't make me feel better."

"So who was the hot guy who let me in before he left? Big, handsome absolutely to-die-for."

Mari groaned. "Brody. Oh, Daisy. I really messed up." She told her what happened with Brody.

"Wow. Just. Um. Do you think that was the right thing to do? I mean the guy was cleaning up your kitchen when I arrived. Are you sure you want to let that go? And if you do, can I have him?"

If looks could kill, her sister would be dead.

Daisy held up her hands in surrender. "Jeez. I'm kidding. Back down. But I mean, the guy helps you fix up your house. Mom texted me and said she and dad were really taken with him. And then when I got here, he told me he was really grateful. He asked me to look out for you. That doesn't sound like a guy who wants to break up."

Mari shoved his letter toward her.

"Hmm." Daisy set aside the piece of paper. "Hold on a minute."

Her sister left and came back with a small wooden starfish and a card. On the back of the starfish were the words *Mari's floor*. He'd whittled her a sea creature from a piece of her wood flooring.

A lump formed in her throat. It was the most thoughtful gift ever.

"When he was leaving, he first ran across the street and returned with this. He put it in your office and then told me not to say anything. That you'd find it when you were ready."

Why would the man do something so sweet when

she'd basically told him to hit the road? It took everything she had, but she forced herself to open the card. It was for Valentine's Day. The outside said, *Thank you for teaching me what love is.*

Mari's eyes blurred and her hands trembled as she tried twice to open the card.

> Mari, while I haven't been able to say the words, I do feel them. You've taught me so much the last month. My heart is yours.
> I love you,
> Brody.

She sobbed. "I'm such an idiot."

Her sister took the card from her hands and read it. "Yep. You're an idiot."

"LIEUTENANT, THE CO wants to see you," Ben said.

Brody slammed shut the manual he'd been referencing. He'd been working on a new test for the grunts and had come in early to get everything ready so that he could take some leave.

His dad needed him, and Brody wouldn't let him down. And his class was doing better. Ever since the picnic, grades had picked up. The grunts were studying harder. His new emphasis on communication seemed to be paying off. Amazing what a barbecue could do. Perhaps there was something to the CO's team-building initiative.

And then there was Mari. He thought if she

read the card that she'd realize how much he cared. Maybe she hadn't been in her office yet. Maybe that's why she hadn't called. He was trying to give her some space, but it was hard.

What did the CO want now? Brody wasn't even supposed to be in today. He was only here to make sure whoever took over the class for the next week had everything they'd need.

Brody contemplated asking for a transfer in the meeting, just in case Mari was serious about the breakup. He wasn't sure he could stand it—staring over at her house every day.

Though it might not be her house for long. He strode down the corridor toward the CO's office. Early this morning he'd noticed the real estate agent's sign in the front yard. It hadn't been there when he'd left her house at midnight.

He knew she had to sell it, but it still irked him. She loved that house. He'd watched her fall in love with it as they completed each room. But she'd told him more than once that she had to get a return on her investment or she'd be in trouble.

Wasn't his problem, she'd made that more than clear. Didn't keep him from worrying about her. The thing with her parents, she shouldn't have to face something like that alone. At least her sister was there.

What he couldn't face was Mari not wanting to have anything to do with him. Maybe his card didn't say what she needed to hear. It had taken everything in him not to go over there and set things straight. When he told his dad what had happened, his father had given him some good advice.

"I'm the last guy to listen to about relationships," his father had said. "But I did get it right once. With your mother. She was the light of my life. My anchor. I've been lost without her. Ever since she died, I've tried to find someone who was my everything, but I'm worried she was it for me."

"How did you know Mom was the one?"

"I couldn't imagine a world without her in it," his dad had said simply.

Wasn't that where he was with Mari? He couldn't imagine his life without her now. But after what had occurred with her parents, how was he supposed to convince her of that? And he'd done his best ever since they'd met to let her know he wasn't the settling-down type.

She thought she was doing them both a favor, but she was wrong.

"I'll let him know you're here. And fair warning, he's in a mood," the CO's assistant said.

Great. "When is he not?"

The guy smiled as he picked up the phone and pushed the intercom. "Sir, the lieutenant's here."

"Send him," the CO grunted.

Keep it together.

"Sir?" He stood at attention.

"At ease," the CO said and leaned back in his chair. "Take a seat."

He'd prefer to stand, especially if he was going to get his butt handed to him on a platter.

"How is Mari? Is she feeling better?"

Brody stared at his shoes. "I guess she's doing okay," he said. How was he supposed to know?

"You *guess*? Eyes up, Marine. Tell me what's going on."

What was he, some kind of psychologist now? It was none of his business.

"Well?"

"She hasn't talked to me since the party," Brody replied.

"But I thought she was simply embarrassed about the roast, which no one cared about. That food you ordered was very good."

Brody cleared his throat. "Sir, it's a personal matter. Other stuff happened with her family last night and she…uh."

"Yes?" The CO shifted forward. Wow. This was never going to end.

"She decided that it might be best to sever ties with me." Sever ties?

"She broke up with you because of something that happened with her family? You didn't do anything?"

"I existed." It was true. He really hadn't done anything but try to care for her. More than he'd ever cared about anyone.

"This *stuff* she went through. Did you offer to help her?"

"Look, sir. She told me to get lost. I didn't think it was a good idea, but I didn't have much choice. She doesn't want me around, so I shoved off. I'm giving her space."

"Brody…" Odd. The CO had never used his name before. "What you've relayed was probably true at first, but like anything you really want, you have to fight for it with everything you've got. And in my book, you have a tremendous amount. I know I've been rough on you, but I believe in you. So should you."

Brody was stunned. "But she won't talk to me."

"Do you care about her?"

"Sir, you don't seem the type to…put your nose in other people's business. This doesn't affect how I'm doing my job, so I don't understand why you feel it's important to—" He wasn't sure how he was going to finish that sentence. He was going to get demoted. Served him right.

The CO shoved a finger toward him. "Marine, I'm not meddling. I'm trying to figure out why one of the best men on my post is requesting a week's leave just as we're coming to the end of grunt training?"

"Sir, my reasons for the leave have to do with my dad."

The CO stared at him.

Brody sighed. "He has cancer. He needs me to go to Houston with him so they can run more tests. It's a bad situation, sir. And I don't want to go, but my dad—" His voice caught. His dad was scared. He'd realized that during one of their many conversations over the last twenty-four hours. "It's the first time he's asked me for anything." Well, other than to babysit his stepsiblings. But this was different.

"Well, certainly I'll approve the leave and if you require more time, let me know. Make sure Corporal Petersen has everything he needs to give the final test."

"Yes, sir, already on it."

"One more thing, Brody. When you were with Mari, you really buckled down. You became a leader. Your students worked effectively as a team. She is what you needed to become a better man. So figure out how to make Mari feel better because women like that don't come around often. You let her slip through your fingers and I guarantee you'll regret it. I made that mistake once, and if I could go back and change it I would."

The man wasn't wrong, but what could he do about it?

"Marine, we never leave a man behind. Never. When she needed you the most, you let a few harsh words drive you away. What kind of man does that make you? Not the man I was thinking about promoting."

No. "Sir, bringing my private life onto the base isn't fair. I'm good at what I do."

The CO took a deep breath. "You're an exemplary Marine. But you need to work on your leadership skills. The man who helped that woman create the house of her dreams. The one who led that couple around so that they might hire her later. The one who used diplomacy to get the people who had hurt her out of the house so that she could heal—that's the kind of man I'd consider for command on this post. Do you hear what I'm saying?"

Brody was about to lose it when it hit him. He'd left her alone when she was hurting the most. He should have taken her and held her. Should have soothed her. Should have told her she didn't know what she was talking about.

He loved her. He couldn't live without her. And he wanted forever.

"I'm a fool," he whispered.

The CO chuckled. "Yep."

"Sir, there's something I've been meaning to tell you. You're right about me not being fit for command. I lied to you."

"What do you mean?"

"When Mari and I showed up at the picnic, she wasn't really my girlfriend. She just came so you'd think I'd settled down. And honestly, to get Carissa to leave me alone."

The CO steepled his fingers and stared Brody down.

Now I'm in for it.

"I see. I'm glad you were finally honest with me. But Lieutenant, you've looked like a man in love from that first day, and let me be frank with you, you aren't that good of an actor."

Had he been in love with her since the beginning?

"What am I going to do?"

"I suggest pulling out the big guns."

"I have to go, sir. I have to fix this." Brody saluted and made for the door.

"Marine?" Brody turned back around, but he was already halfway into the corridor. He had so much to do.

"Sir?"

"No matter what happens you've got the promotion."

That should have been the best news ever, but there was something he wanted so much more.

"Thank you, sir. Really."

Then he was out the door. Pull out the big guns.

He had an idea and took out his phone. Years ago his mother had left him something and he'd never had cause to use it. But he did now.

When his father answered, Brody said, "Dad, I need your help."

16

On day three of her Brody detox, Mari felt awful. Head fuzzy from too much wine the night before, she nearly missed her office chair as she tried to sit down. It rolled with her weight, and the small movement made her feel nauseous.

Elbows on the desk, face in hands, Mari tried to come to terms with the fact that she'd made a mistake. Made a mistake in the worst way. And she didn't know how to make it right.

"What did you do? You look terrible," Abbott said as she came in and sat down in one of the white upholstered chairs across from the desk.

"Shhhhh."

"Nasty. Whatever happened must have been bad. Really, really bad."

Mari nodded. She spilled all the details. Every stupid thing that had happened.

"I can't believe I missed that. I knew I should have stayed in town." Abbott whistled.

"Shhhhh," Mari begged again. "Whisper."

"Wait," Abbott said in a loud stage voice. "So he wanted to make a commitment and even said he loved you. But you decided since your parents couldn't make it work, there's no way you could ever be happy in a relationship?"

"When you say it like that it's even more tragic. Daisy has been pointing it out to me all weekend. He showed up yesterday when I was doing the walk-through at the Caldwell house. I can't believe I missed him. And Daisy told him that I wasn't available. I'm sure he thought I was there and wouldn't see him.

"So then I went to his house and he didn't answer. I called the base and they transferred me to his CO. He said Brody was now on leave and out of town. He wasn't sure when he would be back. I asked him twice if he knew where he was, but he couldn't tell me. I had a feeling he wanted to, but they probably have rules about that sort of thing. Or maybe he's not really on leave. Maybe he's just gone and the CO wanted to let me down easy."

"Oh, no. Do you think he's being transferred?"

Mari felt like she could vomit again. What a fiasco.

"He cares about me. He's a great guy. And I dumped him in such a rotten way, I don't think he'll ever forgive me." Why did she let the past mess with her head?

She had the right to be happy.

Abbott smiled. "Well, I'm not so good with relationships, but he needs to know that you love him. I'd think that might be a good start."

Yes, it would. But when would Brody be home? She wanted to text him, but how would that look? The same with a phone call. No. It had to be face-to-face. She wanted him to see that she was ready for whatever he might be ready for.

But first, before she could move on with her life, there was a special task she had to do. She sat back at her desk and called her mom.

"I wasn't sure I'd ever hear from you again," her mother said hesitantly. "At least not anytime soon."

Mari sighed. "I'm still having a tough time with what happened. But I wanted to tell you something."

"Okay," her mother said.

"I love you."

There was a sniffle on the other end of the phone.

Mari's eyes watered. Her parents hadn't been able to tell her the truth, but they'd also given her a wonderful childhood.

"Darling girl, I love you, too. We should have been honest with you from the beginning. It's, well, there's really no excuse. And we were terrible to have dumped it on you that night. You've always been so independent, it never occurred to either of us that you'd idolized our relationship."

"I did. Daisy and I both did, Mom. You guys seemed so perfect."

Her mother sniffled again. "We were friends. We

still are. It took us a long time to figure things out and then even longer to actually admit it. I know that you said you didn't want us in your life anymore, but please know that your father and I love you with all of our hearts."

Mari swallowed the huge lump in her throat. "It's not all your fault, Mom. You did try to tell me, and I've been so selfish, so wrapped up in my own drama, I wasn't ready to listen to anyone about anything the last few months."

"Baby girl, if you'd let us, we would have been there for you. Your sister, your father and myself. We only want you to be happy."

"I know," she said. And she did. Never once through all of this had she doubted her parents loved her. "So, Mom, you know how when I was kid I used to tell you everything? Even stuff you didn't want to hear?"

Her mother laughed. "Uh-oh. What did you do?"

"It's bad, Mom. It's really, really bad."

THE NEXT WEEKEND, Mari was at the office trying to drown her sorrows in work. It wasn't happening. She still hadn't heard from Brody and wasn't sure if she ever would.

Her phone rang. It was Abbott. "What's up?"

"Where are you?" Abbott asked. "You told me to meet you at your house this morning. We were going to check the plans for the Campbells' kitchen."

She smacked her palm to her forehead. "I came

in early to fix the budget for the Morrison job and totally forgot." She'd forced herself to get in her car because she knew she had to stop staring out the living room window at his house.

Where was he? The longer they were apart, the more her heart ached.

"Huh. It looks like your neighbor is home."

She nearly dropped her phone.

"What?"

"Brody's doing something in his garage. He keeps glancing over here."

"What are you doing?"

"Standing outside your front door talking to you."

He was home. And he was looking at her house.

"Abbott, go sit in your car. Whatever you do, do not let him leave. I don't care if you have to block his driveway with your car. Do you hear me? If you love me, you won't let him leave."

"On it," her friend said.

This had to work. Had to.

Almost an hour later, Mari pulled into her driveway and nearly crashed her car into the garage. The brakes screeched as she jerked to a stop. The sold sign mocked her from the front yard.

When did that happen?

Why hadn't Abbott told her?

There had been multiple offers, and she'd asked her agent to take the highest one. But she hadn't expected it to happen so fast.

She glanced around for Abbott's car. Where was her friend? And Brody's garage was shut. Was he home?

Tears burned and threatened to fall down her cheeks. Pushing her way out of the car, she stood and stared at the old Victorian. Sold. She should be happy. The financial burden would be lifted.

But it hurt. Heart-ripping-out-of-her-chest bad. The house she and Brody built would now belong to someone else.

It felt so final. This was it.

The grocery bags in her hands slipped to the ground, while the sobs came fast and easy. She'd screwed up. So much. What if he didn't forgive her? Making him a meal, which had been her big plan, didn't seem like enough.

"Mari? Honey, are you okay?" Brody was beside her. His arm wrapped around her shoulders. "Did something happen? Are you sick?"

He was here. Touching her.

And she couldn't speak. Just shook her head. And then pointed to the sold sign.

He glanced to where she gestured. "Oh. Yeah. I thought you'd be happy about that."

The tears fell again. "No," she managed to say. "Ours."

He smiled. Why did he have to be so wonderful? Why didn't she just let him stay with her? She savored every second she had with him. They could have had a lot more.

"So you're upset that the house sold? Because it was something we did together. We made it a home."

She nodded.

"That's good to know. It makes what I'm about to say a little bit easier."

Whatever it was, she didn't want to hear it. He'd probably been deployed. She might never see him again. Panic tightened in her stomach.

I might never see him again.

He watched her carefully. "I don't know what's going on in that head of yours, but I need you to let me say this. Please."

His smile disappeared.

Whatever it was, it was serious.

"Wait," she said, hiccupping. "Where have you been?"

He cast his eyes down and then back to her face. "My dad has cancer. I've been at MD Anderson in Houston with him while he had some tests."

"Oh, no. Is he all right?" Now she felt like the most selfish jerk in the world. His poor dad.

"He will be. It's a tiny tumor on his liver. The docs think it's benign, but we won't know until they do the surgery."

"Brody, what can I do? If you need someone to stay with him, I can get away from work. My job is a little more flexible than yours. And Abbott can handle the walk-throughs."

He smiled then and caressed her face. "Always trying to take care of everyone. I missed you."

"Brody, I'm so sorry about everything. Most especially, I'm sorry I took it out on you."

"I know," he said carefully. "There's something else I need to say."

She could take it. She deserved whatever he dished out.

"I bought the house for you, Mari. It's my gift to you for showing me what love is. What it can be." He reached for her hand and held it in his.

"You…what? How?"

He shrugged. "Someone who loved me a long time ago left me a gift, and I felt like this was the best way ever to pay it forward."

"You bought the house?" She sounded silly repeating the words, but she couldn't fathom it.

"I can't promise that I won't get transferred. And once I'm back on active duty, I may get deployed. But I do love you. No matter where I am, you will always be in my heart. Even if you tell me to go right now. Still, I'm hoping that for the rest of my life you'll be there. There's no greater joy than seeing your beautiful face every day."

Choked up, Mari leaned into him. "You don't believe in forever."

"No. That's where you're wrong. I didn't believe in forever, but I do now. I just had to find the right woman. A woman who makes forever possible, and honestly Mari, I can't imagine living my life without you."

It was too much. This had to be a dream. It

couldn't be real. "But I'm such a wreck, how could you even think about forgiving me?"

He chuckled. "I'm right there with you, same as you. And there's nothing to forgive. If anything, this bump in the road showed me that I will do anything to have you by my side. Please say you'll take this journey with me. I'm not sure what the future holds, but I do know I don't want any part of it if we're not together. We can figure it out as we go along. Please just say yes."

"Yes," she cried. "Yes."

He kissed her then and she wrapped her arms around him.

"Take me home, Marine."

"We are home, babe. As long as you're in my arms, I'm home. I love you."

She kissed him. "I love you. I will follow you wherever you go because you're right, home is wherever we are together."

"I'm going to take you inside that jaw-dropping house and make love to you."

"Brody?"

"Yeah," he said as he scooped her up.

"Since it's our house now, I think we should re-christen all the rooms."

A slow smile crept across his face.

"I really love the way you think."

* * * * *

COMING NEXT MONTH FROM

Available March 22, 2016

#887 ONE BLAZING NIGHT
Three Wicked Nights
by Jo Leigh
To get past Valentine's Day, new friends Brody Williams and
Marigold McGuire are pretending they're in love. But their
burning-hot chemistry means the Marine and the interior
designer's make-believe is quickly becoming a supersexy reality...

#888 HOT ATTRACTION
Hotshot Heroes
by Lisa Childs
Reporter Avery Kincaid is determined to uncover the truth
about the wildfire that almost killed her nephews. But gorgeous
Hotshot firefighter Dawson Hess is out to distract her...in the
sexiest way.

#889 SEDUCING THE BEST MAN
Wild Wedding Nights
by Sasha Summers
Patton Ryan and Cady Egerton have nothing in common except
their need for control. And their out-of-control attraction for
each other. Will protecting those they love bring them together,
or tear them apart?

#890 A DANGEROUSLY SEXY AFFAIR
by Stefanie London
Quinn Dellinger was determined to get the promotion she
deserved at Cobalt & Dane Security. Then she saw the guy who
actually got the job: former FBI, completely ripped...and the man
she slept with last night.

REQUEST YOUR FREE BOOKS!
2 FREE NOVELS PLUS 2 FREE GIFTS!

Ⓗ HARLEQUIN®

Blaze®

red-hot reads!

YES! Please send me 2 FREE Harlequin® Blaze® novels and my 2 FREE gifts (gifts are worth about $10). After receiving them, if I don't wish to receive any more books, I can return the shipping statement marked "cancel." If I don't cancel, I will receive 4 brand-new novels every month and be billed just $4.74 per book in the U.S. or $5.21 per book in Canada. That's a savings of at least 14% off the cover price. It's quite a bargain. Shipping and handling is just 50¢ per book in the U.S. and 75¢ per book in Canada.* I understand that accepting the 2 free books and gifts places me under no obligation to buy anything. I can always return a shipment and cancel at any time. Even if I never buy another book, the two free books and gifts are mine to keep forever.

150/350 HDN GH2D

Name _____ (PLEASE PRINT) _____

Address _____ Apt. # _____

City _____ State/Prov. _____ Zip/Postal Code _____

Signature (if under 18, a parent or guardian must sign)

Mail to the **Reader Service**:
IN U.S.A.: P.O. Box 1867, Buffalo, NY 14240-1867
IN CANADA: P.O. Box 609, Fort Erie, Ontario L2A 5X3

Want to try two free books from another line?
Call 1-800-873-8635 or visit www.ReaderService.com.

* Terms and prices subject to change without notice. Prices do not include applicable taxes. Sales tax applicable in N.Y. Canadian residents will be charged applicable taxes. Offer not valid in Quebec. This offer is limited to one order per household. Not valid for current subscribers to Harlequin Blaze books. All orders subject to credit approval. Credit or debit balances in a customer's account(s) may be offset by any other outstanding balance owed by or to the customer. Please allow 4 to 6 weeks for delivery. Offer available while quantities last.

Your Privacy—The Reader Service is committed to protecting your privacy. Our Privacy Policy is available online at www.ReaderService.com or upon request from the Reader Service.

We make a portion of our mailing list available to reputable third parties that offer products we believe may interest you. If you prefer that we not exchange your name with third parties, or if you wish to clarify or modify your communication preferences, please visit us at www.ReaderService.com/consumerschoice or write to us at Reader Service Preference Service, P.O. Box 9062, Buffalo, NY 14240-9062. Include your complete name and address.

HB15

Samantha O'Connel grabbed her phone. "What?"

"Huh. That's one way to answer the phone."

It couldn't be—

Matthew Wilkinson. Matt? *Matt!*

Sam hadn't heard his voice in a very long time.

Her eyes shut tight as the world stopped turning. As the memories piled one on top of another. He was her first love. And her first heartbreak.

"Hello? Still there?"

"Hu…hi, Matt?"

"How are you, Sammy?" he asked, his voice dipping lower in a way that made her melt.

No one called her Sammy. It made her blush. "I'm… fine. I'm good. Better."

"Better? Was something wrong?"

"No. I meant to say richer."

He laughed. "I'd kind of figured that after reading about your work."

Her face was so hot she was sure she was going to burst into flames. She was a jumble of emotions. "How are you?" she asked instead.

"I'm good. Jet-lagged. Just in from Tokyo."

"Godzilla stirring up trouble again?"

"I wish," he said, his voice the same. Exactly the same.

She wanted to curl up under the covers and dream about him. "Nothing but boring contracts to negotiate."

"But you still like being a lawyer?"

"Some days are better than others."

"And you're living in New York?"

"I am," he said, the words delivering both disappointment and relief. If he'd moved back to Boston, she would've died. "I heard from Logan last night. He said that crazy apartment of yours is not to be missed."

Hi there, worst nightmare! She held a groan. "We haven't talked since you…"

"That's true," he said smoothly. Then he sighed. "I've thought about you. Especially when I've caught yet another article about something you've invented."

She smiled and some of her parts relaxed. Not her heart, though. That was still doing cartwheels. "I'm still me," she said.

"Look, I'm coming to Boston for a few days, and I'd love to stay in that smart apartment. But mostly, I want to see you."

See her? Why? "Um," she said, because she couldn't think straight and this was Matt. "When are you coming?"

"In three days."

No. The word she was looking for was *no*. She couldn't see him. Not in a million years. It would be a disaster. "Yeah. I've got some deadline things, but, you know."

He laughed. Quietly. Fondly. And that was what made him so dangerous. He was rich, gorgeous and could have any woman on the planet. The problem was that she'd fallen in love with him two minutes after midnight on her birthday.

"I'm excited to see you, Sammy…"

Don't miss ONE BLAZING NIGHT by Jo Leigh,
available April 2016 wherever
Harlequin® Blaze® books and ebooks are sold.

Whatever You're Into… Passionate Reads

Looking for more passionate reads from Harlequin®?
Fear not! Harlequin® Presents, Harlequin® Desire and
Harlequin® Blaze offer you irresistible romance stories
featuring powerful heroes.

✦ HARLEQUIN *Presents*.

Do you want alpha males, decadent glamour and jet-set
lifestyles? Step into the sensational, sophisticated world of
Harlequin® Presents, where sinfully tempting heroes ignite a
fierce and wickedly irresistible passion!

✦ HARLEQUIN *Desire*

Harlequin® Desire novels are powerful, passionate and
provocative contemporary romances set against a backdrop of
wealth, privilege and sweeping family saga. Alpha heroes with
a soft side meet strong-willed but vulnerable heroines amid a
dramatic world of divided loyalties, high-stakes conflict and
intense emotion.

✦ HARLEQUIN *Blaze*

Harlequin® Blaze stories sizzle with strong heroines and
irresistible heroes playing the game of modern love and lust.
They're fun, sexy and always steamy.

Be sure to check out our full selection of books
within each series every month!

www.Harlequin.com

THE WORLD IS BETTER
WITH
Romance

Harlequin has everything from contemporary, passionate and heartwarming to suspenseful and inspirational stories.

**Whatever your mood,
we have a romance just for you!**

Connect with us to find your next great read, special offers and more.

DK EYEWITNESS TRAVEL

TOP10
TORONTO

LORRAINE JOHNSON
BARBARA HOPKINSON

Top 10 Toronto Highlights

The Top 10 of Everything